PROMETHEUS REBOUNDS

PROMETHEUS REBOUNDS

A FABLE OF HOPE

BILL DANKS

CONTENTS

DEDICATION

For Andrea, Dawn and Shaun

"What one man can imagine, another can achieve."

—Jules Verne

"Nothing is too wonderful to be true."

—Michael Faraday

"I know there are forces out there that bring suffering to others and misery to the world.
But I want to be the opposite force;
I want to be the force which is truly for good."

—John Coltrane

CHAPTER ONE

STRANGE THINGS KEPT HAPPENING TO HIM. UNEXPLAINED THINGS. WEIRD and wild things. Sometimes even kind of wonderful things, but still strange things all the same. He had no idea why they kept happening. He'd never really wanted much out of life except to be left alone and to maybe someday do something right for a change, something that would count, something special. Not that he'd ever thought of himself as anything special. In his own mind he was just your typical eighteen year-old Japanese-American/ Greek-American guy named Prometheus Go who loved basketball and hated homework. That's exactly what he was doing that day. Playing the one, avoiding the other.

It was a late Spring day in Philadelphia. Still cool and crisp and perfect for shooting hoops. Not that he considered any day less than perfect when it came to basketball. They'd had the playground to themselves since four-thirty when the last school bus left. There were six of them. The others were all younger than him. At five-ten and a hundred and sixty-five pounds, he was also the biggest player on the court. Not to mention the absolutely best rebounder.

All that was about to change.

He had just fired off an incredibly long shot and his eyes were following the ball on its flight to the basket. When he turned his attention back to the court he saw that everybody was leaving. Miguel and Su-Cheng and Hakeem were actually *running* away. Juanita and Kim were backing off more slowly and coolly, but there was no question that they too intended to abandon the court. Then he saw why.

It was an invasion. Hordes were streaming in through both the front and back gates. College boys. Led by that great blonde beast Durk Viktor himself. Six-foot-five. Two hundred and thirty-something pounds. Heavily muscled like some kind of wild mountain gorilla that must have pumped iron all day long. Bright yellow hair cropped within a quarter-inch of his massive skull. Wearing the finest tan in all the universe, or at least the finest money could buy at the finest tanning salons in the Greater Philadelphia area. Smiling his wonderfully evil full-toothed smile that revealed a huge mouthful of glittering, gleaming, glistening perfectly pure white caps.

"Afternoon, Jap," he shouted pleasantly.

Prometheus turned away and pumped off another long shot. It missed. Durk laughed.

"We're ready to play now, Jap."

"So play already," countered Prometheus.

"So get lost already, Jap."

"But I'm not quite finished yet," Prometheus explained carefully with an innocent smile.

In a flash Durk closed the distance between them, pulled the ball away, and started dribbling with it. "Yes you are."

He laughed louder, really playing up to his boys now. That was all Prometheus needed. He swatted the ball out of Durk's hands and dribbled it quickly as he circled behind Durk towards the basket. The shot he took then was even longer than before. Better yet, he sank it. Nothing but net.

"Not bad," conceded Durk.

"I know."

"Listen, I'm sorry . . . about callin' you a Jap, I mean."

Now Prometheus laughed. For some strange reason that seemed to bother Durk. He actually looked kind of pained as he slowly shook his head from side to side.

"No, really. You're no Jap. Is he, guys?"

They all stared at their leader for their cue. When he shook his head again they did the same.

"See . . . everybody agrees with me. You're no Jap at all. You're only—"

His long gorilla-like arm shot out as he easily plucked the ball back from Prometheus.

"—half a Jap," he concluded, quickly slapping Prometheus across the face.

That was it. He had taken plenty from Durk over the last few years, but never an actual slap before. He couldn't let it pass. He charged, throwing his right fist straight at the center of Durk's grin. It should have shattered several of the beautiful teeth there. It should have decked him. Hell, thought Prometheus, it should have killed him. Instead, Durk just blocked the punch with the ball. Easily. Two of his boys then grabbed Prometheus and held him back from trying again.

"I'll kill you!" Prometheus screamed.

"Nah . . . ," drawled Durk, "you couldn't do that. In fact, I bet you couldn't even kill me in a friendly little game of one-on-one."

"Try me!"

"Okay. For what . . . say, a hundred?"

Durk pulled a single crisp bill from his pocket. Prometheus had a grand total of twenty-three cents in his.

"I don't carry around that kind of money."

"Tough, kid. I don't play for nothin'."

"I can get it," Prometheus said, thinking of his little sister's piggy bank.

"Jap, I never ever play for credit. But, say . . . I've got an idea. Maybe there *is* something you could put up against my big old hundred."

"Name it."

"Well, since you're always hanging around here getting in my way, let's say that if you lose today you stop doing that. In other words, anytime you see me coming to play, you just hand me the ball and leave. How's that?"

"You got it," Prometheus told him, " . . . if I lose."

Durk laughed. His boys laughed. They let Prometheus go and they moved off the court. His arms had barely been freed when Durk suddenly fired the ball into his gut. It knocked him down. He could hardly breathe. He felt the salty start of tears in his eyes. Then he heard that damn laughter again. Louder than ever. He was still hurting but somehow he managed to roll over, get back on his feet, and start dribbling towards the basket. Durk was right behind him trying fast to crowd him out, but despite all his pain Prometheus was still just a bit quicker. He shot. It scored.

"Two points!" Prometheus screamed in Durk's face.

Prometheus figured Durk should have been mad. He should have been mad as hell. Anger should have filled that big ugly tanned face of his. He should have cursed him. Instead, he just laughed and shook his head again.

"Okay," he whispered, "two points. There won't be many more of those."

They played.

Prometheus quickly scored again. And then still again, but after that the course of the battle began to change. Durk's speed and agility were no better than his, but his strength and endurance were. So was all the experience he'd gotten playing college ball. It wasn't very long before Prometheus simply couldn't keep up with him. Durk was too big. Too tough. He kept overpowering him and was soon scoring twice as often. Prometheus tried to avoid looking at him. Not just because it was more important to concentrate on the ball, but because he just didn't *like* looking at him.

Durk was scary. Even though he was white there were times Prometheus thought he somehow must be the evil twin of Charles Barkley. That famous unforgiving grin that says, with all the confidence of the cosmos behind it, "you're mine, chump, you've always been mine, you'll always *be* mine, so why are you such a fool to even play with me?" Yeah, just like Barkley . . . except for one thing. Prometheus knew that beneath it all Barkley was still actually human.

On the final basket Durk used his shoulder to knock Prometheus over. Then he went on to slam-dunk the winning point. His gang roared. Prometheus went over to the fence to collect his books. None of his friends were in sight. Not even Juanita. He was glad of that.

"Remember now," Durk called after him, "*anytime* you see me coming from now on."

Prometheus left the school yard. The walk home seemed long. Longer than it had ever seemed before, even though it was exactly the same half-mile as always. He shuffled along hardly noticing the tourists crowding the streets. Barely responding to neighbors greeting him in Mandarin, Cantonese, Hakka, Vietnamese and Korean. Barely noticing all the deliciously pungent smells of duck and shrimp and beef and pork and all that wonderful pan fried chow mein that filled his street. He didn't really look up until he entered the doorway of the tiny restaurant with its big red neon sign flashing: "GOLDEN APPLES OF THE SUN . . . THE FINEST JAPANESE-GREEK CUISINE IN ALL CHINATOWN."

The place was packed for once but only two waitresses were on duty to handle the crowd. The taller one was Gaia, his mother. She used to be a model. "Centuries ago," she always kidded, but he couldn't imagine how she had ever been more beautiful back then than she was now in her forties. Of course models didn't have to have their long red hair pulled up into a tight bun beneath a white cap as they carried heavy trays of sushi and baklava between the crowded tables. She nodded at him and smiled.

"You're kind of late, aren't you?"

"Yeah," he admitted.

"We've been busy . . . for a change," she whispered.

"Sorry, mom."

He took his books back to the kitchen and quickly got into his white bus-boy's uniform. When he came out again his sister Athena spotted him and waved from across the room where she worked at the cash register. Though only twelve years old, she was as quick and efficient on the machine as anyone they'd ever had. Plus she actually knew how to repair it, which no one else ever did.

Just then Prometheus sensed the other waitress approaching from behind him. This was his aunt Emiko, at twenty-three the youngest of his father's five sisters and it was often said the prettiest of them all if she'd only smile. What Emiko said was that she wasn't the least bit interested in such reactionary sexist notions as pretty. She tried proving her point by never smiling and by the severity of her short spiked haircut with its wide splashes of orange and green covering nearly half her natural black.

These actions had proven to be only partially successful. True, none of the men who came in ever thought of her as pretty. The black ones and the white ones just stared in awe at the curves of her trim body beneath the tight uniform, and at her smooth round face with its huge dark almond eyes. They thought of her as sexy.

The Asian ones listened in wonder to that strangely nasal sound of her whining Philadelphia accent as she took their orders for food and declined their invitations for dates. They thought of her as exotic.

Prometheus thought of her as a pain-in-the-ass.

"So where the hell *you* been so long after school?" she demanded. "Don't you know how friggin' busy we've been this afternoon? Your poor mom's been out of her mind worrying about you. I swear to God, you kids today ain't got no— "

His mother came up behind her and gently placed a hand on her shoulder. "It's okay, Emiko."

He used the opportunity to escape towards the pile of dirty dishes on a recently vacated table over near the door. Still, he got to hear Emiko's parting shot zinging its way after him. One word only. The usual. "*Bakata!*"

Yeah, he thought to himself as he cleared the dishes, that's me all right. A real fool. Things hadn't been going right ever since his father had died. That was two years ago now. He knew his mom was worried about keeping the restaurant, but there just didn't seem to be anything he could do to help. Whenever he offered to get a job, a real full time job outside the restaurant, she exploded and told him he was going to college and that was that. Case closed.

After a couple hours of busing tables he went back to the kitchen to take a break. He was about half-way through a Pepsi when Gaia came in. She pointed at him.

"I don't want you sitting back here drinking sodas."

"Don't I get a break?"

"No. No break."

"But mom, that's not—"

She smiled. "Go upstairs and do your homework."

"What about the restaurant?"

"Jason just arrived and the dinner crowd is finally thinning out. You can leave now."

"All right!" he shouted, quickly finishing the soda and tearing off the uniform. He grabbed his books and headed for the door to the back alley.

"*All* your homework," Gaia called after him.

"Of course, mom."

"Good-night."

"Good-night, mom."

Sure, he thought, he *would* do his homework. Really. *All* of it too. Eventually. But not right then. He could think of better things to do. One in particular. The entrance to their apartment was just a few doors down the alley from the restaurant. He covered the distance in record time, flew in and out of the building, and was soon headed back to the schoolyard. Minus the books, but carrying his own basketball.

He really needed a little more time on the court. Hopefully Durk and his gang would be gone. If he was really lucky the place might even be deserted entirely. That's what he wanted. To be alone. To just take some shots in peace and have a chance to think.

It hadn't been a great day. First thing in the morning he'd gotten back his final exam in Advanced Placement Calculus. He scored 93 on it. Some stupid mistake in *arithmetic*, of all things, kept him from doing better. Still a 93 wasn't really all that bad. The real problem came in second period when Mrs. Kennedy returned his final English paper. Prometheus received a B-minus. His lowest score ever. He dreaded telling his mother. Not that it would be such a tremendous surprise. He'd been sliding downhill all semester in English. Gaia wouldn't see any excuse for that. To her there didn't seem to be any excuse for anything.

So he already had that B-minus on his mind when the trouble with Durk began. He was all that Prometheus needed. Durk and his gang and the usual racist cracks. The kind of thing that had been building up over the years. He never understood why.

There had been a time when Durk wasn't like that at all. Prometheus remembered him as a star high school player that every kid in the neighborhood looked up to. He wasn't just great at basketball either. He genuinely seemed like a nice guy back then, even helping younger players learn the game. Then something must have happened after he started college, but Prometheus had no idea what it might have been. He only knew that whatever it was had completely changed Durk.

Somehow everything came together in that one quick disastrous game with him and that stupid bet that Prometheus had made and lost. Then those dull hours cleaning up after customers in the restaurant. No, not much of a day at all so far.

He tried putting all that out of his mind as he reached the schoolyard. A full moon had come out and the night had turned quite chilly. The downtown city air smelled nice and clean for a change. Prometheus finally started relaxing a bit as he felt himself filled with the love he had for his mother and sister. He chuckled as he realized he also loved the Chinatown neighborhood where he had gown up. Hell, he was even willing to concede that he might actually even love the whole wickedly exciting city of Philadelphia itself.

There wasn't a soul in sight and he had his basketball. It looked like the day might at least *end* okay.

Then a strange thing happened.

CHAPTER TWO

PROMETHEUS IMMEDIATELY BEGAN SHOOTING BASKETS ON THE POORLY LIT court. Or rather, he began trying to shoot baskets. For some strange reason the ball just wouldn't go in. Shot after shot kept missing. Even at fairly short distances he simply couldn't score. When he tried a long shot the ball went wild, sailing right over the backboard and landing in a large trash compactor behind it.

He went to retrieve the ball, but stopped short and froze a few yards away. The ball was rising up out of the trash. On its own. Well, not exactly on its own, he soon realized. It was now resting on the top of something. An old hat. An old black pork-pie hat, like something he'd seen in movies of the forties. Then he saw that the hat was also on top of something. It was a very small, very ancient looking black man dressed in a rumpled black suit.

The old man climbed out of the compactor and brushed off all the trash. Then he reached up to his hat and removed the ball. He took it off his hat and held it out in front of him, examining it as if he'd never before seen anything quite like it.

"Don't appear to be anything wrong with the ball," he said in a low gravelly voice that reminded Prometheus of another old movie he'd seen of jazz trumpeter Louis 'Satchmo' Armstrong. "Glad to hear that," Prometheus told him. "Let's have it."

"What?"

"The ball, pops, the ball."

"There's nothin' wrong with it."

"Great. Give it back then."

"I think the real problem is your impatience and anger, son."

"I'm not your son," snapped Prometheus. "Give me my goddamn ball!"

The old man pointed at him with it. "Yep, that's it all right. Anger and impatience. That's why you lost this afternoon."

"You were here?"

"Sure."

"I didn't see you."

"I sure as hell seen you!" said the old man, laughing at the thought. "I seen you lose because you couldn't control yourself."

"Oh yeah? *That's* why I lost, huh?

"Chiefly," the old man said with a quick nod.

"Not the fact that Durk has over a six inch height advantage and more than fifty pounds on me?"

"Size ain't shit, boy,"

"Like hell it ain't!"

The old man smiled and held the ball out in front of him again. First in both hands, then in just one, extending his arm as far as it would go.

"Son, you got at least that same height and weight advantage on me, plus a tremendous age advantage. So why don't you just *take* your ball back . . . if'n you can?"

Prometheus tried. He lunged forward to grab the ball, but in an instant the old man snatched it away and was dribbling with it. Prometheus was angry so he charged him. He didn't care much how old or little the man was. He'd knock him right over like Durk had done to him. But strangely that's not what happened.

In the last possible split/second before Prometheus would have been all over him the oldster pivoted away and fired an impossibly long shot straight into the basket.

"Three points," he said.

They both rushed to recover the ball, but the old man got there first. He caught it still on the first bounce, then he dribbled it all around Prometheus. Sometimes he came in real close, but Prometheus still couldn't even touch it. He noticed how strangely the old man moved. How gracefully, almost without any physical effort at all. Like a ballet dancer or something. It was actually kind of beautiful to watch. It was definitely something impossible for a person his age.

Finally the old man handed back the ball and bowed. Prometheus lined up a foul shot. However, just as he was about to release the ball, the old man stole it back and shot it himself. The move was perfect. Over his shoulder without even looking at the basket. It was done with such speed that the chain actually sizzled as the ball flew through it.

Prometheus went over to the curb and sat down with his head in his hands. The old man came and stood in front of him in the street. Prometheus looked up and realized just how really strange he looked. Everyone always talked about white people and black people, but from an early age Prometheus sometimes wondered why—since most real people were actually more pink or brown.

But not this old timer. He really *was* black– a pure coal oil midnight black, not brown. The street lamp right above them shone down directly on his face, but it revealed surprisingly little of his features. His face was black like a black hole. It took everything in and reflected very little back.

Then there was the goatee. It looked a bit like the one Prometheus had seen on a record shop poster of the Bop legend Dizzy Gillespie.

One thing the light did reveal was his eyes—or rather *eye*, since the one on the left was covered by a large black patch like something a pirate might wear. The one eye that showed was strange. For one thing it looked much too big for the rest of his face. That made it kind of scary because it seemed like it could see everything around it. Besides that, it was absolutely the bluest eye Prometheus had ever seen.

"First Durk this afternoon," Prometheus complained. "Now you. That had to be magic or something you were using against me."

The old man laughed. "Son, that weren't no magic I did just then, but if it's magic you want . . . . "

He held up his hand and spun the ball on his index finger. Prometheus watched, totally unimpressed. "I've seen that before."

"Have you now?"

"Sure. Lots of times."

"Well then," the old man said slowly, his mouth turning up even further into a gigantic smile that revealed a full set of pure white teeth. " . . . have you also seen *this*?"

He lowered his hand from the ball. It kept spinning. On its own. In mid-air. Prometheus' own eyes widened as much as his.

"That's impossible."

"Why?"

"It . . . it just is. "No one can do that."

"Wrong. *Any*one can . . . if I teach them."

Prometheus thought that over for the better part of a second. "Even me?"

"Sure."

"What would it cost me?"

For the first time the grin left the old man's face.

"Everything," he said solemnly.

"Huh?"

"Basketball is a sacred game. It's a gift stolen from the gods and brought down to earth for the enlightenment of the people here. It demands that you put everything you have into it. It demands an absolutely total commitment."

Prometheus thought it over. "Everything?"

"Absolutely."

"A total commitment?"

"Totally," said the old man, putting his hand back out and plucking the still spinning ball out of the air. He threw it to Prometheus, but it went right over his head and he had to chase it back into the schoolyard. When he caught up with it a few seconds later he turned around again towards the street to question the old man further. He was gone. There was no one in sight for blocks in any direction.

*   *   *

Athena was busy working away at his computer keyboard.

Her granny glasses had slid down and did little to make her baby face look any older, although that had been her intention when she first saw them years before in an old hippy boutique on South Street. Gaia had been firmly set against her daughter wearing them since Athena's vision had always been perfect, but then Athena went to her father who laughingly agreed as long as she only wore plain uncorrected lenses in the antique wire frames. Athena was delighted and commented that the glasses would give her the more 'mature' look she needed to be taken seriously.

Now she was helping Prometheus with his homework and he was taking her most seriously, despite the glasses. He stood behind her. Amazed, as usual.

"You can't do that," he told her.

She laughed. "Watch."

"It's impossible."

"That's what you think, brother."

Her typing continued even more furiously than before. Then she paused dramatically and raised her right hand high over the keyboard. She grinned as she slowly brought the hand down again to make a final keystroke. That did it. The monitor screen started flashing colors and bells rang out several distinct tones. A whistle sounded from one of the speakers.

"You did it!" Prometheus shouted.

"Naturally."

"You're brilliant, little sister . . . brilliant but dangerous."

"Give me access and I can rule the world," she said with a laugh as she flipped her long red hair that so resembled her mother's and was in such contrast to Prometheus' much shorter black hair. People often thought that strange because although both children took after their father to some extent, Athena's face looked even more Asian than her brother's, which had a greater resemblance to Gaia's.

Just then their mother came in. She stood watching them for a moment before she said anything. She had been doing that a lot lately.

"Athena, are you bothering your brother again?"

"No."

"Yes she is, mom," he said, tickling his sister.

Athena giggled as she pulled away from him. "No! No!"

"How's the homework coming along?" asked Gaia.

"Almost done," Prometheus said.

"Mine's all done," added Athena.

Gaia stared at both of them again, for an even longer time than before. She smiled and came over to hug them. "Your father would be so proud of you two."

"Why?" Prometheus asked.

"Well, for one thing the way you're both doing so very well in school."

"Oh, that?" He hadn't yet told her about the English paper or the Math grade.

"Yes . . . *that*, my geniuses. I know it hasn't been easy with him gone."

"I'm no genius," he said.

"*I* am!" Athena quickly shouted.

He nodded. "You know something, mom, she may be right. I've never seen such a natural on the computer."

Gaia hugged them again. "Well, you taught her."

"But now she's teaching me."

"*See!*" Athena said, sticking out her tongue.

"Okay, okay, so I've only given birth to one genius . . . or maybe just one little smart-ass, but either way I think it's time you go to bed, young lady."

Gaia and Prometheus each held their breath, but if Athena hesitated at all it was only for an instant. Then she rose from the computer, kissed them both, and headed for the door. "Good-night, mom. Good-night, big brother."

As soon as she was gone Prometheus heard his mother sigh. He knew just how much she wanted to tuck Athena in, but the doctor had advised against it. His sister was making progress but it was taking such a long time. For most of the first year after their dad's death she could only go to sleep with all the lights on and both her mother and Prometheus in the room with her all night long. Then she could handle it with just a night-light and Gaia alone staying with her until she dozed off. It was only during the last few weeks that she had started going to bed by herself. Even now though it was inconsistent. There were those nights when she still needed her mother.

Whenever she asked, Gaia would go, but she'd never volunteer. It appeared to be working.

"She seems happy, don't you think?" Gaia asked. "I guess the psychologist was right after all about her getting over it . . . eventually."

Prometheus had guessed that the psychologist was a fool, a real *bakatari* in his own right, but he didn't want to say anything just then to Gaia. She looked so tired and worn down. It had been a tough two years for her. Tougher even than it was for Athena and him. His dad and mom had been dating since high-school. They'd gotten married when they were still in college. For almost twenty years they'd struggled to make a life, then just as they started to enjoy a little success, dad died. You never ever "get over" something like that, thought Prometheus. You just learn to live with it, to go on somehow. Hell, maybe that's what the doctor actually meant after all.

Prometheus didn't know. He just knew that two nights before he'd heard his mom crying softly in her room. He'd knocked, but she wouldn't let him in. He didn't know if she'd been crying over dad, or just worrying about Athena and him, or about the future of the restaurant, or maybe all of it together.

Now she was hugging him again. "Your father really would be so proud of her."

"I know, mom."

"And he'd be proud of you too, of course," she quickly added.

That was strange. Prometheus couldn't see why.

CHAPTER THREE

PROMETHEUS ARRIVED AT SCHOOL EXTRA EARLY THE NEXT MORNING TO PRAC-tice his foul-shooting, but that turned out to be impossible. The place seemed much busier and louder than usual. There were long tables set up all over the schoolyard. Some students were reading brochures. Others were filling out papers at those tables already manned by teachers. What was going on?

Then he saw Helen Stellanova. She was struggling to get through the crowd with her guitar case in one hand and her books in the other. He went over to help her. She let him carry the books as they made their way over towards the main building.

"What's up?" he asked her.

"It's the summer camps sign-up. Don't you remember?"

"Oh yeah," he lied, " . . . summer camps."

"Aren't you signing up for one of them, Prometheus?"

"No."

"Oh, I thought you might be."

"Nah, no time."

"But the basketball camp . . . some colleges are offering special scholar-ships based on competition held up there. So I thought that you might—"

"I already have a scholarship, Helen."

She looked embarrassed. "I'm sorry. I guess I forgot."

"Hey, it's no big thing."

"Don't say that. Computer Engineering is no big thing?"

Prometheus shrugged. "Depends on how you look at it."

They reached her locker and she put the guitar inside. It barely fit. He handed back her books, said good-bye, and headed off towards his first class.

Then another one of those strange things happened. When he turned the corner at the end of the hall he looked back and it seemed like she was still standing at her locker staring after him. Maybe he was wrong though, because just then she looked down and got real busy spinning her combination lock.

Helen Stellanova staring at *him*? Nah. No way. Not in his wildest dreams. He thought of how she was such an incredibly beautiful African-American/Sicilian-American girl with a high forehead and cheek bones forming a profile so perfect that the gods themselves must envy it. Not to mention a lush figure of truly cosmic significance. Her skin was such a creamy golden brown, her ebony hair so long and silky. Plus she always smelled so good to him—sometimes like jasmine, sometimes like sandalwood, sometimes just like a fresh breeze blowing through Fairmount Park out past the Art Museum. The strange thing was that Prometheus had once gathered up enough nerve to ask her what kind of perfume she wore. That question had really seemed to embarrass her because she looked down and giggled nervously before replying that she never wore perfume. Just as he noticed that she never wore lipstick or any other makeup or nail polish. Or needed to.

Plus she was famous as the only person in the history of the school to ever score a perfect 1600 on the SAT. Plus she was rich. Plus she had already given two classical guitar recitals for which she received rave reviews in all the papers. Plus she was going to record her first CD that summer. Plus she had lived in Paris and spoke French fluently. Plus she drove her own car. That was just too many pluses for him.

Not that he ever thought she was stuck up or anything at all like that. Just the opposite. Helen was the sweetest girl he'd ever known. Despite all her success she actually seemed kind of shy at times. He guessed those big glasses coupled with her small size and soft voice only added to that impression.

It was true that her brother Maximus once said she had a crush on Prometheus. In fact, he said the only reason she stayed on at the public school was because Prometheus went there. He figured Maximus was just putting him on. The real reason she remained there was probably because *Maximus* hadn't. Yeah, that had to be it. She just didn't want to go off to private school with a brother who was always teasing her. What else could it be? After all, somebody like her . . . with somebody like Prometheus? He was better off hanging out with someone like Juanita, someone from the neighborhood who wouldn't get his hopes up and then break his heart. Not that

Juanita and him were anything but good friends yet, but you never knew what the future had in store. What the fates had in mind. He'd never had a real girlfriend. Maybe Juanita would be the first. He knew it couldn't ever be Helen.

*   *   *

Durk and his troops were hanging around after school waiting for the yard to clear, so Prometheus went home early. He figured that should please Emiko for once. When he entered the restaurant, though, she ignored him and just kept waiting on the single customer in the place. It wasn't until he started changing into his bus-boy things that she finally spoke up. Even then she seemed to do so rather reluctantly.

"Your mother wants to see you."

"Where?"

"Back in the kitchen."

Prometheus kept changing. That made Emiko clap her hands loudly and shout at him. Same old Emiko after all. "Now!"

He hurried back to the kitchen. Gaia was busy cooking, but she stopped as soon as she saw him. She motioned for him to sit in the chair near the chopping block.

"Hey, mom," he began defensively, " I came right home after school to-day. No basketball or anything . . . besides, the restaurant's nearly deserted."

That's when another strange thing took place. The worst one so far. She started crying. This time right out in front of him. She never did that before. Not even when Dad died . . . well, not very much anyway. Prometheus asked her what was wrong.

"There was a phone call for you."

"So?"

"It was this morning. Long-distance. From the university. I told them you wouldn't be home until after school. They asked if I were your mother. When I said yes, they gave me a message for you."

"What is it?"

He thought she was going to keep crying, but it was just then that she stopped and came over to stand beside him. She reached out and put her hands on his shoulders.

"It's about your scholarship."

He waited. She didn't say anything more. It looked for sure like she was going to cry again. "What is it, mom?" he finally asked. "What about my scholarship?"

"There isn't going to be one," she answered slowly.

"What are you talking about?"

"It's been canceled for lack of funding."

He still only had one arm in the bus boy's jacket. He felt too tired now to put in the other one. Gaia brushed a strand of hair out of his eyes. "Maybe I can get a loan or . . . "

They both knew that was impossible. There was no way they could even qualify for another loan, let alone afford to pay one back. Every penny was needed just to keep the restaurant open.

*   *   *

"Old man?" Prometheus called, looking in the trash bin but finding it empty. "Old man?"

"My *name* is Hobie," the old man answered, coming up behind Prometheus from the corner of the building which he'd just rounded. "Hobie Wonder. No relation to Stevie though, unfortunately. Damn but that boy can sing!"

He sounded a bit drunk, but just the tiniest bit. He kind of walked like he might be drunk too, but then again he was so naturally loose and dis-jointed that it was hard to tell for sure.

"My name's Prometheus."

Hobie laughed. "I knowed a Prometheus once. A long, *long* time ago. It weren't around here though. No, sir. Nowhere at all around here. This Prometheus was—"

"I want to ask you something."

"Shoot."

"Define 'total commitment'."

In the instant he heard him say those words, Hobie became cold sober. He pointed at Prometheus' chest. "Your very soul, boy."

"Oh . . . "

"What the hell did you expect? Basketball is a form of absolute beauty. To play it right you have to do it with all your soul dedicated to furthering that beauty. Anything less will diminish the real magic in the game. It should never be played just for fun or money or to impress the girls or for any of them other ulterior motives. The primary purpose must always be to put more beauty into this poor tired old world. Do you understand?"

"No."

"Let me show you then."

Hobie stepped in front of him and bent over the trash bin. For a second Prometheus thought he was going to fall head first into it, but he was just reaching down to get something underneath some papers and cans. It took him a few seconds before he found what he was looking for and held it up high over his head in the moonlight.

"What's that?" Prometheus asked.

"It's a basketball, of course!"

It didn't look like any basketball Prometheus had ever seen. For one thing it was blue. A brightly glowing blue. For another thing it didn't really look that much like a ball. At least not at first. Oh, it was round in shape all right, but kind of flat looking, more like a disk than a sphere. The strange thing was though that the more Prometheus looked at it the more it seemed to *become* a ball. It puffed out right before his eyes until it resembled a globe of the earth, only an earth that was all ocean and no land.

"Whose is it?"

"Mine, of course," said Hobie.

"Where'd you get it?"

"Enough questions! Let's play."

They did so. At first Hobie took it easy with him, moving around the court in a pretty relaxed way at only moderate speed. He clearly had no trouble dominating the action, but he was generous and at times he let Prometheus get the ball and take a shot. Some of those shots even went into the basket. He caught Prometheus smiling once when that happened and he told him to keep smiling. He even said that *not* smiling was one of his major faults, one of the main reasons he wasn't a better player.

Then Hobie started speeding things up. Faster and faster. Soon they were moving like Prometheus had never moved before. He didn't think he could maintain Hobie's pace, but somehow he did. The strange thing was that the more aggressive Hobie became the more he was able to match him. They were both going all out, yet it seemed like there was a kind of harmony growing between the two of them. The competition was real. They were constantly scoring on each other, but at the same time it was as if they were working together trying to accomplish something bigger than the game, something that took their combined efforts to do right.

In the end they were both playing at truly blurred speed. Ball after ball went flying through the hoop. Hobie was laughing. Prometheus was laughing. It was one of the greatest moments of his life.

*   *   *

Prometheus figured it might have been a little late when he got home, but without a watch he didn't know for sure. The apartment was dark so he decided to play safe and creep in as quietly as he could. He took off his shoes at the door and slowly tip-toed down the hall to his room. It seemed to work. No sign of Athena or his mother. He left the lights out as he flopped down on his bed in total exhaustion. The game had taken everything out of him. He was beat. He felt great!

Suddenly the night stand light flicked on. Gaia was sitting in the chair by the bed. He jumped up. Startled. Even kind of scared. "Mom!"

"Where have you been?"

"Out."

"Where?"

"The playground," he said.

"Doing what?"

"Playing."

"Prometheus, do you know what time it is?"

"No, not really. Maybe round midnight?"

"Two-fifteen," she told him.

Nah. It just couldn't be. Sure, they had played a while, but it couldn't have been that long. Couldn't have been anywhere near that long. He would have guessed maybe an hour or two tops. No way more than five hours. That was just too strange to be real.

"I know you're upset about the scholarship," Gaia went on, "but just what could you have been playing till after two in the morning?"

"Basketball."

"With who?"

"A friend."

"And *his* parents, don't they care he's out so late on a school night?"

"I kind of doubt it," Prometheus said.

"Well . . . *me*, I care!"

"I know, mom."

"And your father . . . if he were still alive . . . do you have any idea how much *he'd* care?"

"I guess so."

"So what about *you* . . . don't you care now? Or are you going to start staying out all night playing basketball and just give up on your education?"

"Aw, come on mom, I'll graduate. No sweat."

For some strange reason that seemed to anger her more than anything else. She rose from the chair and walked over to stand right over him, pulling her old terry-cloth robe tighter around her body. Prometheus noticed how the frayed and faded fabric seemed so loose on her. She had definitely been losing weight lately. He sat up straighter in bed.

"From *high school* you'll graduate!" she shouted. "Of course no sweat! Not for that. But what about beyond? What about college?"

Prometheus shrugged. "Who knows?"

* * *

The next morning he was in Athena's room helping her pack the huge school-bag she always dragged around with her. He didn't know how she did it. That thing was really *heavy*, even for him. Her actual school things took up comparatively little of the bag's space, but then she stuffed it to the bursting point with thick computer technical manuals and software packages and god knew what else.

"You two better hurry up," Gaia called in from the living room. "It's almost time for Athena's bus."

"I hate school," his sister mumbled.

"Why?"

"It's stupid."

"Hey, don't talk like that," he told her. "School can be very . . . uh, educational . . . uh, very important."

She stopped packing and glared at him. "That's easy for you to say. You won't be going much longer."

"Yeah," he admitted. "I guess you got that right."

He turned around and moved towards the door. Athena must have thought she hurt his feelings because she ran over and blocked his way. Then she took his hand and looked up at him with big sad eyes.

"But listen, brother, if for some strange reason you really *want* to go, then maybe I can help."

"How?"

She pointed across the room to her desk and the computer that sat on top of it. "With that."

* * *

Things didn't always go so well with Hobie. At least not as well as the night they played so smoothly together for five hours. No, there were times when Prometheus just didn't understand him at all. Times when he didn't make any sense. When he was just a weird old dude who seemed like some kind of alien from another world. Some kind of ghost from a forgotten time long ago.

That Saturday afternoon, for example. It was late but they were still lucky to have the court to themselves. Hobie was standing beside him as he practiced his foul shooting. The ball hit the rim and bounced away. Prometheus shook his head. Hobie nodded his.

"Better," Hobie said.

"*Better?*"

"Much."

"It didn't go in," Prometheus reminded him.

"So?"

"So how can it be better?"

Hobie smiled. "You were more relaxed, more well balanced, in greater harmony with yourself."

"Yeah, yeah, I guess that's all well and good, but what I really want is for the stupid ball to go into the basket. Can you dig it? I want to do something . . . *anything* . . . right for once in my life. Anything. Just once."

Hobie went on like he hadn't heard a single one of the words Prometheus had just uttered. "Your arms moved with a better sense of rhythm. Your hands released the ball at more nearly the optimum time. Your fingers were more finely controlled. Your eyes—"

"I missed the shot!" Prometheus shouted.

"So?"

"So it wasn't 'better'."

"It was *much* better, Prometheus. Your eyes were opened wider and in greater focus. Your legs . . . "

Prometheus didn't want to hear any more. Hobie was sounding like Dad. Like that time some five years before. No, it was actually more than six years. He was twelve years old at the time, just about Athena's age now.

*   *   *

His father had taken him along to the archery ranges in the park. Prometheus felt kind of silly and more than a little embarrassed. All around them were these guys dressed in either really dangerous looking combat fatigues with camouflaged markings that blended right in with the trees and bushes, or else the latest sportswear that made them look like Olympic athletes.

And there was his dad walking right past them in his white *gi*. Not that the *gi* itself was all that bad. It was the same kind of outfit worn for judo or karate. With his black belt around his waist his father actually looked kind of cool. The problem was that he wasn't there to *do* judo or karate. He was there to do *Kyudo*, traditional Japanese Zen archery, and for that he had added something to the basic *gi*. What he had added was the *hakama*, and what the *hakama* actually was . . . was a long black cotton . . . *skirt*!

So Prometheus was walking along past all these tall, young, rugged, macho, dressed-to-kill archers, and by his side was his father— a little old balding man dressed in a skirt!

Prometheus wanted to die. No, he wanted more than that. He wanted to just disappear completely. To not be there at all. To not exist. He was sure there was going to be trouble. Someone was bound to start making fun of his father. Calling him names. Taunting and teasing him. Trying to push him into a fight. It was inevitable. He just knew it was going to happen. How could it not? They were all staring when he and his dad went by. Some were starting to grin. A few were even nodding.

And yeah . . . here it came . . . right on schedule . . . the biggest of the bunch . . . headed right for them . . . barrel chested and bearded . . . looking like he could have been Durk's older and hairier and even larger brother. Prometheus wanted to run. But it was too late. The hairy giant's interception course had been well plotted. It brought him out onto the path right in front of them. He stepped forward and looked at Prometheus' father and . . .

And then a strange thing happened.

The huge man bowed deeply. Then he spoke to Dad in a deep rumbling voice . . . in *Japanese*.

"Konnichi-wa, Go-sensei."

Dad bowed and returned the greeting. Then they switched to English as they proceeded to discuss bows and arrows. Prometheus was going nuts. What the hell was happening? How did this brute know Dad's name? Why had he called him "teacher?" Dad wasn't a teacher. He just ran a little restaurant.

Before that he'd driven a taxi. And why was this guy so interested in Dad's archery equipment? After all, it was nothing more than a simple old bamboo long bow with simple old bamboo arrows. Nothing special at all.

It was the other guy's stuff that was fascinating. He had that really expensive looking hi-tech compound bow with all those wheels and pulleys and complex criss-crossed wires and weights and counter-weights and even some kind of fancy sighting mechanism. Plus he had the baddest arrows in the universe. They were made of black metal with long four-bladed razor heads. Prometheus thought he could probably kill most anything with them. The man and his friends had been shooting at large targets shaped like moose and bear and even lion. Dad's arrows, on the other hand, just had plain old ordinary rounded target points on them.

A good five minutes or so went by before their discussion finally ended. They bowed again at each other, then Prometheus and his father continued on down to the end of the field where a few of the smaller sized black-and-white *Kyudo* targets were set up.

Dad did a few stretching exercises, then he strung his bow, nocked an arrow on the string, pulled it back to full draw and held it there for a moment.

"Balance," he whispered to Prometheus. "Balance and relaxation and harmony, these are the essentials."

Then he did something strange. In the very instant he released the arrow he turned his head *away* from the distant target at which he'd been aiming.

"Bulls-eye!" Prometheus shouted in utter amazement a moment later.

"So?" asked his father.

He was still facing in the opposite direction.

"Your shot, dad, it was perfect!"

"It was that," his father said calmly, "even before the arrow reached its mark, even before it left the bow."

"But you hit the bulls-eye. Dead center."

Finally he turned, but only to face his son, not the target. "Prometheus," he said gently, "that is the very *least* important aspect of the shot."

"But you scored a bulls-eye without looking at the target!" Prometheus insisted. "You always hit it."

His father smiled. "So?"

"And I never do."

*   *   *

Hobie had the ball now. He held it loosely on the fingertips of his out-stretched left hand. Prometheus watched as he slowly turned the ball over and over again in the breeze.

"Such beauty, such harmony is the very truth, the very essence of the shot. Whether or not the ball actually goes into the basket or not . . ."

Hobie casually tossed the ball in a slow high arc towards the backboard more than half a court away. Then he turned and walked off in the opposite direction, saying as he went, " . . . is nothing more than an afterthought."

The ball sailed right into the net without even touching the rim. Prometheus shook his head and frowned. Was this kind of strangeness spreading or what?

CHAPTER FOUR

WHEN PROMETHEUS GOT HOME ATHENA WAS PLAYING THEIR FATHER'S old *Koto*, a Japanese table harp. Her long pigtails flew from side to side as she speeded up the tempo. He laughed and tried humming along with the tune.

"I remember that song."

"Do you remember this too?' she asked, stopping her song and picking up a *Syrinx* lying beside her. She tossed it over to Prometheus.

"My old Pan Pipes! I thought I threw it away."

"You did, brother, but I took it out of the trash."

"Why?"

"So we could play together again someday . . . like today."

"But I *can't* play," he reminded her. "You know what Dad said."

"Aw, c'mon . . . ," she insisted. "join me."

He really didn't want to, but maybe it might be good for her if they played a little together again. This was the first time he'd seen her touch any of Dad's things since he died. Yeah, it would be excellent for her.

He ran his fingers along the smooth bamboo, tracing the Greek letters at the base of each tube. He always thought the *Syrinx* was a great instrument. He remembered the story his mother had told about how it was named after a beautiful nymph who fled from the god Pan into the swamps and was changed into a clump of reeds. Pan was heartbroken. He cut the reeds and tied them together forming the pipes that sometimes bear his name as well as hers. Prometheus used to love the way his mother told that story. She used the *Syrinx* to dramatize it as she went along.

It was a great instrument all right, but an extremely difficult one to play. Much harder than say a regular flute or recorder. After all, they had holes and keys that you could finger. The *Syrinx* had nothing but open tubes. Like blowing into a bottle, everything depended upon the player's own lips and the angle at which his breath attacked the wood. Very few people could really play it well. Dad, of course, was a master of the instrument as he was of most things. Prometheus wasn't.

As Athena and he began to play he remembered another time, years before. He was trying his best on the pipes and she was then playing a smaller scaled-down version of the *Koto*. Dad was expertly strumming the full size instrument. He was also giving his son instruction.

*   *   *

"Prometheus! You must relax and breathe more deeply."

He kept trying but he kept failing. He knew his posture was too rigid and his tone too pinched, but there just didn't seem to be anything he could do about it.

"Bring forth the inner beauty of the bamboo!"

"How?" Prometheus asked.

"*How*? Just let it flow from your soul."

He tried that, but it just made matters worse. Again he knew how badly he was failing to please his father as the old man looked over at Athena, winked, then turned back to Prometheus and smiled.

"You do *have* a soul . . . don't you, Prometheus?"

He wanted to throw the instrument down and just walk out. He wanted to so much that day, but of course he didn't.

*   *   *

But now, in the present with Athena alone, he did exactly that. She looked bewildered, picking up the *Syrinx* and calling after him. He didn't turn back.

*   *   *

Luckily Hobie was still at the court and it was still deserted. They started working on rebounds. It was then that Prometheus learned how the old man's politics were just as strange as the rest of him.

Prometheus's attention was distracted by a poster on a nearby phone pole. The poster was of a popular state senator who was running for re-election in the Fall.

"Why are you looking at that fool?" demanded Hobie.

"He's not a fool," Prometheus snapped back. "My Social Studies teacher says he a great man."

"Why's that?"

"Because he's sponsoring a lot of really important and much needed legislation."

"Like what?"

"Well, uh . . . for one thing he wants to bring back the death penalty."

Hobie started coughing so violently that Prometheus was actually afraid he was going to choke to death himself. Then it suddenly cleared and the old man shouted hoarsely at him. "He wants to goddamn *what?*"

"Bring back the death penalty."

"And you call that 'great'?"

"Uh . . . yeah. What would you call it?"

"What I'd call it, boy," Hobie answered with a wicked grin, "not to put too fine a point on it is . . . shit."

"Why? Don't you know that there are criminals who have done things so vicious that they deserve to die?"

"I know it better than you do, son."

"Then what's wrong with the death penalty?"

"What's wrong is the matter of just *who* would administer it and the extraordinarily dangerous power they gain in being able to do so."

"What do you mean?"

"Just that if the government has the power to kill the guilty, then they have the power to kill the innocent. If they can kill some, they can kill any . . . and will!"

"I'm not sure I follow that Hobie, what—"

The old man was shaking a finger at the political poster. "Tell me, what other 'important and needed legislation' does this here 'great' politician-man plan on pushing through if folks see fit to return him to office?"

"Well . . . uh, new gun laws for one thing."

"Gun laws?" gasped an astounded Hobie.

"Sure. Now you've certainly got to admit that's something we really need."

"I certainly do not!" Hobie said just before he spit into the street.

Prometheus looked bewildered. "So you think we have enough gun laws already?"

"No, sir . . . we have far far too many of them already!"

"Oh yeah? Well, just how many do you think we should have?"

"That's simple," said Hobie. "We should have none at all."

The old man laughed as his student's face actually seemed to turn red as he sputtered to say something in reply. "N . . . none . . . at all? Why, that's just crazy, just—"

"All right," said Hobie, "if you've just got to have some kind of a gun law, then I guess I can think of one that might make some kind of sense."

"Good. What is it?"

"*Don't shoot people!*"

"Well . . . sure, okay, that makes sense . . . but it's hardly—"

Hobie was shaking his head and frowning. "No, come to think of it that won't do either, because then we'd also have to have a knife-control law that would say don't knife people, then a rock-control law saying don't throw rocks at people, and a baseball bat-control law telling folks don't hit each other over the head with bats, then a chainsaw-control law—"

"Okay, okay," said Prometheus. "I get the point."

"Do you, boy? Do you really get the point that all we actually need is a law that simply says don't attack the innocent. In other words, use force only in self defense."

"But we already have laws like that, Hobie . . . lots of them. Laws against murder and attempted murder and assault . . . and assault and battery . . . and rape . . . and—"

"My point exactly," Hobie said as he tossed the basketball to Prometheus.

"You're strange, Hobie."

"I'll never deny that. In any particular way?"

"Yeah. You're against the death penalty so that would make you left-wing, yet you're also against gun laws which makes you right-wing. Which are you really?"

Hobie laughed louder than Prometheus had yet heard him."Boy, I guess I'm to the left *and* the right of a lot of folks . . . but when you really come down to it, I'm not either 'wing' of that vicious old bird of prey."

When they resumed play everything was great. Prometheus didn't need to be told he was making progress this time. He *knew* it. Rebounding had always been his greatest strength, but now he felt he was really starting to master the art. Which was good because he felt it was about time he mastered something.

Just then Helen passed by carrying several shopping bags. He fumbled the ball. She stopped by the fence and watched them play. He messed up what should have been an easy rebound. Helen smiled. He tripped. She waved. Hobie stole the ball and Prometheus couldn't get it back. The old man dribbled it over towards the fence.

"Who's your friend?"

"Oh . . . uh, this is Helen."

"Whose face 'launched a thousand ships'? Hi, Helen."

She looked embarrassed.

"Helen," Prometheus said, "this is Mr. Wonder . . . Hobie Wonder."

"Pleased to meet you, sir," she said softly.

He shook her hand, then bowed down and kissed it. She looked even more embarrassed. He smiled and pointed at her bags.

"Been doin' some heavy shoppin', I see."

She nodded. "Just some things for camp."

"Which camp is that?" he asked.

"The Symphony Summer Camp."

"Ah . . . what do you play?"

"Guitar."

He threw Prometheus the ball. "Wonderful! Gonna be another Segovia, huh? Or maybe another Julian Bream or Liona Boyd or John Williams or Christopher Parkening?"

"Hardly," she answered. "I've only been playing a few years."

"So? Wasn't there a time when each of *them* had only been playin' a few years?"

"Well . . . yes, of course," she began, "only—"

"Tell me something, Helen, that camp you're going to . . . is it the one up there on the lake, right across from the Collegiate Basketball Camp?"

"Yes."

"Well, you're sure goin' to a fine place. You been there before?"

"Yes, for the last three summers."

Hobie's eye had widened. For some strange reason it seemed to be absolutely twinkling. He kept nodding his head as he spoke to Helen. "Mighty fine . . . mighty fine. Say, I hear that basketball camp is pretty good too."

Helen smiled shyly. "That's what everyone says."

"You know what," said Hobie, "I bet Prometheus could probably learn a lot up there."

Her own eyes started to widen then, and her smile no longer looked so shy. "Oh yes! He really could—." But then she hesitated, glanced quickly from Hobie to Prometheus and then back again to him as she picked up her shopping bags. "Uh . . . I've got to get home now."

"Keep practicin'," Hobie called after her as she quickly walked away.

Strange. Prometheus didn't get it. Hobie and he went back to the basket and resumed their work on rebounding, but now the old man slowed down the pace quite a bit from what it had been before. It seemed he wanted to talk.

"Nice girl."

"Yeah."

"She your sweetheart?"

Prometheus had to laugh. "*What?*"

"You know . . . your girlfriend, your fox, your chick . . . your 'main squeeze' as I once heard it put."

"Nah."

"Why not?"

"No time," Prometheus said, sinking a basket and recovering the ball before Hobie could get it.

"Son, you got a lot to learn."

"So teach me."

"I ain't talkin' bout basketball."

"What then?"

Hobie swatted the ball away from Prometheus. "Oh . . . things that there's *always* time for."

"It's not just that," Prometheus said. Then he related all of Helen's many 'pluses' and how they put her too far beyond his reach.

That just made Hobie snicker. "If the girl's all that great, and I kind of sense that she just might be, then you should strive to become worthy of her. It will be well worth the effort . . . for the both of you."

Prometheus noticed that Hobie was dribbling even more loosely and leisurely than usual, so he thought he'd take a chance even though it rarely seemed to work. He rushed him and made a mad grab for the ball. Amazingly he *got* it! Even more amazingly Hobie failed to block him as he dribbled around him, took a quick shot, and scored. They both laughed at the same time.

"You *are* gettin' better," Hobie said.

"Thanks."

"But I think I know somethin' that just might make you a whole lot better still."

"What?"

"That basketball camp."

"Why?"

"They'd teach you things up there . . . things you really need to know."

"I got you to teach me."

"Don't count on it."

That worried Prometheus. He *was* counting on it. He was counting on it more than anything. Hobie said the price of learning from him was everything, a total commitment. Prometheus had agreed to pay that price. Now he was being told not to count on it. He asked Hobie just what he meant.

"Son, it's just that I don't plan on bein' around here much longer."

Now Prometheus was really worried. "What's the matter? Are you sick or something?"

"Worse, I'm old."

"So you mean . . . "

"So I mean I'm old . . . and tired. I need a vacation. I want to get away from here for a while . . . maybe for the whole summer."

The concern vanished. Prometheus guessed his relief kind of showed. "Oh, I thought you meant—"

"What?" Hobie asked suspiciously. "I sure hope you didn't think . . . " He laughed uproariously. "Hell, I ain't *that* old. I don't plan on *ever* bein *that* old!"

"Good."

"But with me goin' away, that there camp should be just the thing for you. I know one instructor up there who could really offer you something special."

Prometheus didn't want to hear any more. "Say, Hobie . . . speaking of something special . . . you know I feel bad about not being able to pay you anything for these lessons."

"I told you I don't need money!"

"Do you need to eat?"

"What's your point, boy?"

Prometheus told him about the restaurant, about the cards they gave out sometimes as a promotion. How they were good for a complimentary meal of one's choice.

Hobie accepted a card.

*   *   *

Athena was excited. She pulled Gaia and Prometheus into her room. Her computer was already on. The monitor screen was filled with complex mathematical equations.

"Come on, come on!" she urged them.

"What is it?" asked Gaia.

"You'll see."

Athena ran to the keyboard, did some quick typing, then stood back proudly as new equations appeared. Gaia looked at her son for an explanation, but he was as puzzled as she was.

"There!" said Athena.

"What is it, honey?"

Athena nodded at Prometheus. "Brother?"

He checked out the screen. Carefully. Thoroughly. The math was beyond him. He shrugged. "I have absolutely no idea."

"Really?"

"It's out of my league. You'll have to explain it."

"Okay, okay," she said, nearly bursting with pride. "*This* is how Prometheus can go to college."

"What?" he asked.

"And how Mom can sell the restaurant and never have to work again."

"What are you talking about?" Gaia asked.

"*Games!*"

"What kind of games?"

"Games of chance, Mom. You know . . . Las Vegas . . . Atlantic City . . . *gambling!*"

"Honey, don't talk non—"

"Wait a minute," Prometheus interrupted. He was looking at the monitor again. It hadn't made any sense at first, but the more he stared at the equations the more he began to suspect something. What was there should have been as far beyond Athena as it was beyond him. Further, in fact, since he was in the 12th grade and she was only in the 7th. But there it was. Plain as it could be on the screen. He picked up a notebook and wrote in it just to double check what he was seeing.

"What is it?" asked Gaia.

"Just a minute, mom," Prometheus said, still checking, " . . . just another . . . my god, I can't believe this."

"Will it work, brother?"

He nodded.

"Will *what* work?" Gaia now demanded impatiently.

"My gambling program, of course. We can go to Las Vegas or Atlantic City or wherever and make a fortune."

"Not so fast," he said, still checking her figures.

Athena was frowning now. "But you just said it would work."

"It will. At least I think it will . . . . but only theoretically."

"What's that mean?"

He had to figure a way to let her down easily, but he'd never been much good at doing things like that. Athena had flopped down on her bed and was playing with one of her innumerable stuffed animals. A pink gorilla this time. Gaia sat down beside her.

"It's like this," he began, "your programming is fine . . . more than fine. It's perfect. It's absolutely incredible, but—"

"Would we win or not?"

He nodded again. "Oh, we'd win all right . . . in the long run, if we bet enough times."

"How many would be enough?"

"I'm not sure," he replied, pretending to rework the figures again in the notebook, "but I'd guess something on the order of say . . . hundreds . . . of millions."

She looked dejected. He went over to the bed and sat beside her and their mother. "Hey, don't look so sad. This is fantastic work! You really *are* some kind of genius, sis."

"I know," she said matter-of-factly. "I'm only sorry that my program can't make us any money today."

He tried tickling her to make her laugh, to make her smile even, but it had no effect. She just snuggled closer to Gaia.

"Just don't give up," he told her.

"Oh, don't worry about that," she said. "I never *ever* give up."

It was only then that she finally smiled again.

*   *   *

Another strange thing. Hobie came for a meal the next day. Not that that was so strange in itself. After all, he had taken the complimentary meal card, but the way it turned out . . .

It was kind of early for dinner. No other customers were in the place. Athena was at the cash register totaling up the last of the late lunch receipts. Gaia was cooking in the kitchen. Prometheus was cleaning the toilets. The bell jingled over the front door and Athena yelled that they had a customer. Gaia called that she'd be right out. Prometheus had just started mopping up with pine oil when he heard Hobie through the open rest room door talking to his sister.

"Prometheus sent me. He gave me this card."

"Hi. I'm his sister Athena."

Prometheus peeked out. Hobie bowed deeply to Athena.

Prometheus almost expected him to kiss her hand like he'd done with Helen, but he didn't.

"Pleased to meet the goddess of wisdom," he said more than half seriously.

She giggled. "Listen, Prometheus is—"

Just then she caught a glimpse of her brother gesturing that he didn't want to come out. Prometheus had decided that it might prove interesting to hear anything the old man might say about him if he wasn't there. It was something that Prometheus had sometimes done with his father.

"—uh, at the library studying. I don't know just *when* he'll be home . . . exactly."

Hobie stared at the sculpture by the cash register. It was a cheap plaster copy of "Prometheus Bound." Athena picked it up and handed it to him. He held it carefully like a great work of art. It had cost two dollars at a garage sale.

"Weird, isn't it?" said Athena. "It's called Prometheus Bound. That's the same Prometheus my brother's named after."

"I know," Hobie said.

"Do you know the story too?"

"Tell me."

Athena led him to a table. Gaia hadn't come out yet so Athena proceeded to set it up with silverware, a menu, and a napkin as she related the myth of her brother's namesake. Hobie paid strict attention as if she were reciting sacred scripture.

"Prometheus was a Titan. That's a kind of a giant super-hero. In fact, he was almost like a god . . . except that a lot of the regular gods hated human beings."

"And *he* didn't?" asked Hobie.

"Oh no, not Prometheus. He liked us and felt kind of sorry for us. Those other gods didn't want people to have fire, but Prometheus stole fire from heaven and brought it down to earth so that people could keep warm and cook their food and—"

"Be able to see through the darkness?" Hobie suggested.

Athena considered this, then smiled. "Yeah, I guess that too. Anyway, Prometheus got in big trouble. The other gods, especially their boss, found out and they punished Prometheus."

"How?"

"Just like in the sculpture," she said, pointing back at the cash register. "They chained him to a rock and everyday a giant eagle came and pecked away at his liver."

"That must have hurt," commented Hobie.

"Sure it did, and since Prometheus was immortal his liver would always grow back at night. Then the eagle would come for him again the next day."

Just then Gaia called in from the kitchen and told Athena to get some water for the customer. Athena left to do so. Then the strange thing happened. Hobie was staring at the sculpture and his face filled with pain. Real pain. Not just some belly-ache or anything. Although at first *that's* just what Prometheus thought it was because Hobie seemed to be holding his stomach and trying to rub away the agony. Only when Prometheus leaned out for a better look did he realize it wasn't his stomach. It was his liver.

*　　*　　*

Later that night they were playing some free style one-on-one. No real rules. Just make the basket. Prometheus didn't let Hobie know he had been in the restaurant at the same time as him. Athena had whispered the word to Gaia not to reveal him. They both must have thought it kind of strange, but they kept his secret. Now out there on the court Prometheus didn't want to ask Hobie why he'd been holding his liver like that. There was something more important that he wanted to discuss with him. Hobie gave him the opening when he commented again on how Prometheus was definitely getting better.

"Maybe so," Prometheus said, quickly slipping through one of the many long shadows the dull moonlight left on the schoolyard court, "but I'm sure not picking up any of that magic you said I could learn."

"Ah . . . so it's the magic you want?"

"Of course."

"Well, then I guess I'll just have to tell you the secret."

"*Secret?*" Prometheus asked.

"Sure. There's a definite secret to the magic and I think you're just about ready to learn it."

"What is it?"

Hobie had just gotten the ball and was moving away towards the basket, but now he stopped and carefully put the ball on the ground. He walked over to Prometheus, looked around like he was making extra sure no one else was in sight, then he whispered in Prometheus' ear. One word only. "Practice."

That really angered Prometheus. It was exactly the kind of thing his father used to do. Build you up, then let you down . . . drop you off a mountain after he'd led you up to the summit.

"Aw, come on, Hobie . . ."

"What?"

"There's got to be lots more to it than just that."

Hobie smiled. "You're right. There is."

"Well . . ." Prometheus demanded after a long moment of silence, "what is it? To get the magic what else do I have to do besides practice?"

Hobie reached out and touched Prometheus with his index finger. It felt hot against his forehead. This time Hobie gave him two words. "Be good."

Prometheus raced him for the ball. They reached it in the same instant, but Prometheus knew Hobie would be the one to scoop it up first and take off with it. He had the ability. He'd shown that countless times. For some strange reason though he decided this wouldn't be one of them.

Not that the old man made it easy. Prometheus managed to get the ball in his hands, but then Hobie was all over him, blocking every shot he tried to make, constantly threatening to take the ball away, anticipating his moves like he could read his mind. Prometheus had to fight for that basket harder than he'd ever had to fight for anything. When he finally made it Hobie smiled and patted him on the shoulder.

"Prometheus, I've been thinking about that basketball camp again."

"Forget it. It cost too much."

Hobie shook his head. "Don't ever let money stand in the way of something important to you."

"That's easy for you to say."

"It surely is," he agreed with a chuckle. "More than you can ever know. How *much* is too much?"

"I don't know. At least a couple hundred a week."

"Find out the exact figure."

"Why?"

"*Why?* Because I told you to . . . that's why!"

"It won't matter."

"Just do it!" Hobie insisted.

"Okay."

"Tomorrow. First thing. Don't forget."

Prometheus didn't. But it turned out strange.

CHAPTER FIVE

THE TABLES IN THE SCHOOLYARD WERE STILL SET UP THE NEXT DAY, BUT THE lines had almost disappeared. Most of those who wanted to sign up for camp had already done so. Prometheus had the basketball table all to himself. Behind it sat a young teacher he'd never seen before.

"Name?" she asked without even looking up.

"Uh . . . I just have a question."

"So do I. What's your name?"

"Prometheus . . . Prometheus Go, but I—"

"Social Security number?"

"I just want to find out how much the camp cost!"

That did it. She finally glanced up and looked him over. Her glasses kept slipping down her nose. "Three hundred and fifty dollars per week. There's a ten percent discount if you sign up for all eight weeks and pay in advance."

"Wow! That's an awful lot," he said.

She scanned some more papers on the table in front of her, then she smirked. "Obviously not too much for someone like you. You're paid up in full for the whole summer."

"No I'm not."

"Take a look," she said, pointing to a line on one of the papers. "Cash transfer made late last night."

"Who made it?"

"It doesn't seem to say," she mumbled, checking the papers once again.

"This doesn't make any sense."

She shrugged. Then she handed him a thick packet. "This contains your receipt, plus information on scheduling, transportation, and everything else you need to know."

"What I need to know," he said, "is who could've done this for me. Who even knew that I—"

* * *

Gaia cried when he told her the story and showed her the packet. She said she just knew something good was going to happen. She always did believe in miracles. That's how she saw the camp. As a miracle. As another chance for her son to get into college. The packet detailed the very thing Helen had mentioned to him— how there were special scholarships given to the players who really excelled in the summer basketball program. Of course Gaia would have preferred him going to college on an academic scholarship, like the one he'd had, but the important thing was the *going*. Now there was at least the possibility that that might still happen.

Then Prometheus told her he really didn't *want* to go to the stupid camp. She stopped crying. She looked at him like he was crazy. Didn't he realize this was the last chance he had of going to college, at least for that year? That's when he told her he didn't know if he really even wanted to go to college at all. For just an instant he thought she was going to hit him. She'd never done that before. Neither had his father. But right then, for a split/second he really thought it was a distinct possibility. Then the moment passed and she started crying again. Much more softly and quietly this time. With her face turned away from him.

It was Emiko who hit him. Hard. With her open hand across the back of his head. She screamed too. And cursed. And stomped her foot and shook her fists at him. It was strange. He thought she'd kind of be on his side since the reason he didn't want to go to camp or college was so that he could stay home and help out in the restaurant.

That didn't impress her at all. First, she said, he never really helped out all that much even when he did put in time at the restaurant. Second, she argued that if he *really* wanted to help out he'd go to camp, then to college, and then make something of himself. Third, she said how nice it would be to simply get rid of him for a few months . . . or years.

Athena, on the other hand, confessed that she'd miss him terribly if he went away, but even she still thought he should go. So it turned out to be unanimous. He was going to camp. But there was somewhere else to which he was definitely going to go first.

*   *   *

A few little kids were trying to shoot baskets when he arrived back at the playground. He didn't see Hobie so he asked the kids if they'd seen an old man hanging around . . . a strange looking one-eyed old man dressed entirely in black. The kids all giggled. They had no idea who he was talking about. He was just about to leave when he thought of the trash bin. Sure enough, there was a note taped to the inside of the lid. It read, " have a good time at the camp. I sure as hell intend to have one on my vacation."

Prometheus just couldn't figure him. Hobie was the strangest person he'd ever met. There were times when he thought that magic of his must be some kind of illusion or hypnosis or something. It just couldn't be real. Everybody knew there's no such thing as that. Real magic. Yet, there were times like now when Hobie had obviously done the impossible, and there were other times—especially when he got out that mysterious blue globe that he insisted was a basketball—when Prometheus was convinced that Hobie's magic was just as real as anything else in his life. Certainly as real as school or Emiko's constant complaints or Helen's beauty or Athena's brilliance or his mother's love . . . or his father's death.

Yeah, Hobie Wonder was strange all right. Prometheus had pretty much given up on trying to learn much about him personally. Where he was from, or what kind of work he'd done, or even just how old he really was. Most of the time he'd just evade any of the questions like that. On those rare occasions when he did reply his answers were so strange and confusing that Prometheus never really gained any useful information from them. So he'd resigned himself to just accepting the fact that Hobie *was* . . . whatever it was that he was . . . and that Prometheus was lucky enough to have him.

Or rather *had* been lucky enough to have him, since he was gone now and not likely to seen again for the entire summer. If ever.

*   *   *

Things happened pretty quickly after that. Prometheus graduated near the top of his class. The top was Helen. Naturally. She had surprised everyone by turning down the offer to be class Valedictorian. When asked for an explanation she said it was because she didn't have anything important to say. Prometheus thought she was just being modest like she always was. Plus she was probably too shy. The strange thing was how she could play her guitar in public for any size audience, but still seemed afraid to hardly ever even open her mouth in class.

Gaia threw a combination graduation/going-away party for her son in the restaurant after hours. Everyone from both the Greek and Japanese sides of the family showed up. They all chipped in with food and drink. Prometheus got lots of gifts. Most of them were money. He tried giving that to his mother for the restaurant, but she wouldn't hear of it. At her insistence all the money went into the bank earmarked as his special "college fund." She was convinced that he'd really get one of the basketball scholarships. He wasn't convinced of anything at all.

He was afraid to invite Helen to the party, but he had all his friends there from the neighborhood. That was probably for the best. They fit in just fine with the loud music and dancing and drinking and eating. Most likely Helen was off having her own party out at her mansion or wherever it was she lived. Su-Cheng and Miguel combined their resources and gave him a new basketball to take to camp. ElRoi gave him a Sixers shirt a size too big and said he expected Prometheus to grow into it over the summer. Juanita gave him a real silver chain. When he protested that it was too expensive, she winked and said he could return the favor next year when *she* graduated.

Then she gave him another gift. A kiss. A *real* kiss. If it was any kind of standard, he felt it was the *first* real kiss he'd ever had. It made him want more. Lots more.

"When you get back," she said.

She smiled sweetly as she straightened her long soft blonde hair which had become tangled in his awkward fingers. Then she turned and left.

That was strange. He wondered what she meant. It was a promise he guessed. And hoped. Still, he didn't quite understand. About girls, that is. He never did.

Like Emiko . . . she was always putting guys down, giving them a hard time, making fun of them, talking trash about them behind their backs and right to their faces. Yet she came to the party with a boy friend. The first one Prometheus ever knew she had. He seemed a nice enough guy, but nothing really outstanding or unusual. His name was Apollo Ballado. He was kind of tall and a few years older than Emiko and quite Latin looking with his shiny black hair and long mustache. Most surprising of all, he was a cop. Prometheus thought the guy seemed awfully quiet, especially compared to his aunt. What was the attraction?

But then *she* was completely different around him. Unbelievably a little more quiet herself. And definitely more pleasant. And even friendly. She gave Prometheus an expensive pen and pencil set and actually hugged him and kissed him on the cheek as she wished him good luck.

Strange.

CHAPTER SIX

THE NEXT MORNING WAS A REAL SCORCHER. PROMETHEUS WAS UP EARLY AND shooting baskets with his new ball at the playground. He'd been at it for a couple hours and his clothes were soaking wet when Maximus drove up and parked his pickup truck at the curb. He waved to Prometheus as he got out and walked through the gate onto the court. "What's up, bro?"

"Just trying out my new ball," said Prometheus. "it's a gift I got at my party last night."

"You had a graduation party?"

"Sure."

"And you didn't invite my sister?"

"Uh . . . no, I figured she was having her own party."

Maximus frowned as Prometheus passed him the ball and he started dribbling it towards the basket. "No way."

"Helen didn't have a party?"

"Oh, mom and dad and I took her out to dinner, but that was all she wanted. She didn't want to do anything else or have anybody with us."

"But she has lots of friends," Prometheus said, trying to block the much taller and lankier Maximus.

"That's not true."

Maximus made the basket and Prometheus grabbed the ball. He dribbled it back down court, moving it quickly to keep it away from the younger player.

"You know something," said Maximus, "there was someone else besides us . . . a kind of friend, I guess, who I think Helen probably did want to be with last night."

"Who's that?"

"You."

Prometheus nearly dropped the ball just as he was about to make his shot. Instead he just stopped and held it against his chest. "Me?"

"Of course. She was hoping you'd call her."

"But I—"

"She even got you a gift."

"Oh no! I never thought to get her anything."

Maximus gently took the ball out of Prometheus' hands. "It's not too late, you know?"

"What do you mean?"

"Come on out to our place for a swim. It's a hot enough day for it. I'll just tell Helen that I saw you playing here and you looked so sweaty I felt sorry for you and just had to bring you home."

"She'll buy that?"

"Yeah," answered Maximus with a grin, "she'll buy it . . . as long as I have you with me."

"I'll have to get her something."

"That would be a good idea."

*   *   *

They left the playground and Maximus drove Prometheus back to his apartment for a quick shower, a change of clothes, and his swimsuit. On their way out of center city they stopped at a store where Prometheus picked up a dozen white roses and a big box of chocolates for Helen. He couldn't think of anything else to get her. He'd never bought gifts for a girl before and Maximus was no help, insisting that he knew nothing about what his sister might like. As far as he knew she never seemed to want anything.

After leaving Philadelphia by crossing the City Avenue bridge over the Schuykill they were heading into the suburb of Bala Cynwyd when Prometheus realized just how little he knew about Helen and her family. Fortunately Maximus was in a rather talkative mood and started filling him in—first by confirming what he had said once before about his sister staying at the inner city Chinatown school.

The same year that Maximus had won a full scholarship to the exclusive mainline Episcopal Academy, Helen had won a similar scholarship to the equally prestigious Friends Central School. But while he had almost literally jumped at the opportunity, she had firmly insisted on continuing her education in the down town Philadelphia school. She even convinced her parents to fight for an exemption for her to do so since they had just moved out of the area. That had been the same year she and Prometheus first had classes together. So he had been wrong about her staying on just to avoid going to the same new school as her rather annoying brother.

"But I still don't think there can be any connection," said Prometheus.

"Of course there is," Maximus countered.

"What?"

"Boy, you really don't know . . . do you?"

"Know what?"

Maximus laughed. "She *likes* you, dummy! I told you that before."

"But why?"

"Hell if I know. I can't see the attraction myself . . . can't see it at all. You don't appear to be much of a catch in my eyes."

"I know," said Prometheus in a whisper.

Maximus turned the truck off City Avenue and headed down Bala Avenue. A few minutes later they were driving through one of the finest residential neighborhoods in the area. Prometheus stared appreciatively at all the stone mansions they passed. They reminded him of the houses they all used to see on family drives with his father. Someday, his dad used to say, they would leave their cramped Chinatown apartment and live out there in a large suburban home with some ground around it.

"It must be great to be rich," Prometheus commented.

"Sure is, bro. Believe me it is. It especially beats being poor."

"How would you know?"

Maximus laughed. "How would I know? From experience, of course. That's how I know."

"What do you mean?"

"Just that we haven't always been rich. Far from it. The four of us used to live in a center city apartment even smaller than that one of yours I saw today."

"When was that?"

"Just a few years ago."

"What happened then?"

"That's when my dad finally started having some success with what he did."

"In what way?"

*   *   *

Maximus told him the story as they drove ever deeper down the tree-lined streets of the wide-lawned neighborhood. His father Frederico Stellanova had been a teacher most of his life. Chiefly at small Catholic and Quaker schools in the area. The pay was never much but he was good at his job and felt that the work itself was important and rewarding enough to remain with it as long as he could. Often he told Helen and Maximus how overjoyed he was to see how well former students of his had turned out.

Once the family had been stopped on the highway by a State Trooper. They didn't know why. Their father had been driving just as slowly and carefully as he always did. *Too* slowly and carefully, they often kidded him in later years after they themselves had begun to drive and felt that if anything he erred on the side of safety. So why had the Trooper pulled them over?

He came up to their car, all six and a half feet and two hundred some-thing pounds of him, his mirrored sunglasses shining beneath his military-style trooper's hat, his mouth set in a grim smirk below his thick mustache. They were all just a bit afraid as Frederico rolled down his window and asked the officer what the trouble might be. The reply was that there was no trouble at all. The trooper just wanted to say hello to his favorite teacher from so many years before. When he gave his name, their father immediately remem-bered him in great detail, asking how he had been and learning that the man was just finishing law school at night and planning to apply for the FBI the following year.

That was just one.

Another was the beautiful blonde woman with a wonderful smile and a devastating wit who had become the most respected investigative reporter in the history of Philadelphia. She'd had their father as her fifth grade teacher. Yet another was now a neurosurgeon at the University of Pennsylvania Hospi-tal. There were so many more—other doctors and cops, plumbers, a priest, an architect, the exceptionally shy Korean girl who had first started to gain some confidence in herself in his classroom and who now was making a suc-cessful transition from internationally known super-model to an actress of real talent and ability. Then there were the chefs, the construction workers, the firemen, the nurses, the business executives and musicians, computer programmers and taxi-drivers, the book-keepers and salesmen, the clerks and professional athletes.

Most of all there was that tall skinny red-haired girl fresh from Ireland with an accent so thick Frederico had initially been unable to understand even half of what she said. She was now a teacher.

He was proud of them all. Them and so many many others. So many that Maximus and Helen were constantly astounded at just how many he had kept up with over the years, and how many others, like the Trooper, who were constantly popping up to surprise him with ever new joy.

*   *   *

"But how did any of that ever lead to financial success?" interrupted Prometheus.

"It didn't."

"Then what did?"

Maximus slowed down as he made a final turn onto his own street. "Dad has never been just a teacher, much as he loves that profession and excels at it."

"Well, what else is he?"

"An artist."

"What kind of artist . . . a painter?"

"Sculptor."

"All the time he was also teaching?"

"And long before that."

*   *   *

Maximus explained how his grandfather Ruggerio had been a renowned stone mason back in Sicily. He had wanted his son to follow him in the trade, but Frederico never developed any interest in doing so. Instead, there had been a day when he was only about five years old when he watched his father working on a new church in South Philadelphia. It was just a little over a year after they had come over to America. The work of his father and all the other masons on the job was old hat to Frederico by that time. He'd seen it all before in Palermo since the age of two. What he hadn't seen before, or at least ever really paid much attention to before, was the work of the sculptors working near his dad.

From then on Frederico had an all consuming passion for making things with his hands. Drawing. Painting. Woodcarving. Stone-carving. Pottery. He mastered them all while still in grade school. Throughout high school his proud father supported him in spending summers in Italy studying under the finest sculptors in Milan, Florence, Venice, and Rome.

It was early in college while doing volunteer work at a local grade school that he discovered a competing passion for teaching. He soon declared a dual major in art and education. Interestingly, he never had any desire to be an art teacher as such. While it was true that in the classrooms where he taught there would never be any need for an outside art specialist, it was in the basics of reading and writing and math that he devoted his greatest time and energy.

Over the years he kept sculpting and even managed to sell pieces from time to time, but there simply didn't seem to be much of a market for the startling dramatic and realistic figures he produced. That all changed when he entered and surprisingly won a competition held by the Philadelphia Museum of Art in conjunction with the nearby Rodin Museum. The cash prize itself wasn't all that great, but the publicity it generated certainly was. At a special exhibition set up following the competition, every one of his pieces sold within hours. Numerous commissions came his way almost immediately after that. So many, in fact, that he eventually decided to drop teaching in order to fulfill them all.

*　　*　　*

Prometheus realized that they had finally stopped in the driveway of Helen's home. It wasn't exactly the mansion he had thought it would be. In fact it was obviously the smallest house on the block, but it was still a house. A solid stone house. Maybe its pool wasn't as big as any of its neighbors. Maybe it lacked the tennis courts many of them seemed to have. But it was still a house. With its own land all around it. His dad would have loved the place.

"Hey listen," said Maximus just as they were about to get out of the truck. "you know I was only kidding around back there, right?"

"About what?"

"Aw, you know . . . all that junk about you not being such a great catch and not knowing why Helen would ever like you."

Prometheus smirked. "I can't figure that myself . . . if it's even true."

"Of course it's true, and the reason why is really pretty simple if you think about it."

"What?"

"My sister likes you, man, because you're one of the good guys. There aren't that many of us around."

*　　*　　*

The inside of the house was tastefully furnished, but rather sparsely so. Prometheus appreciated its lack of clutter, especially when compared with the cramped apartment where his family lived. It certainly wasn't ornate the way he had often imagined it would be. In fact, if anything the downstairs reminded him of Dr. Okazaki's home which was done in a minimalist Zen style with just a few bamboo chairs and a small low highly polished mahogany table.

There were a few small marble pieces by Mr. Stellanova in the living room and dining room, but actually very few. As there were few paintings on the walls for the home of an artist.

Maximus introduced Prometheus to his parents who seemed genuinely happy to finally meet him at last. They were a cheerful couple, both of them older than Prometheus' parents.

Frederico was stocky and bearded with bushy light brown hair and a wonderful twinkle in his eye behind steel framed glasses. The Sicilian accent of his early childhood was nearly gone from his speech, but not entirely. Prometheus noticed it several times in their brief conversation together before Frederico returned to his studio somewhere in the rear of the house.

Aurora stood just a touch taller than her husband and was quite dark in complexion—not just darker than him, but even darker than Helen. In fact, her color was nearly as dark as Hobie and that was kind of strange because Prometheus thought he had never seen anyone even close to that dark before. He also realized that she was one of the few women he'd ever seen whom he'd consider to be just as beautiful as Gaia. Despite being more than just a few years older than his mother. The lilt of Aurora's native Jamaican speech was still there in her voice, much more evident than was the accent of her husband, although she had lived in Philadelphia nearly as long as he had.

"My daughter is out at the pool," she said as Maximus led Prometheus towards the kitchen and she returned to reading her morning paper.

Wile Maximus poured orange juice into two glasses on a wooden tray, Prometheus stared out the kitchen window at one of the loveliest sights he had ever even imagined.

It was Helen. She stood so tall and proud at the edge of the diving board. Her slender arms were held together out in front of her and her eyes were nearly shut as she readied herself for the dive she was about to make. Her swimsuit was a rather modestly cut one-piece rather than the skimpy little string bikini or thong that Prometheus had often dreamed of her wearing.

Strangely though, it was exactly the same dazzling white color as it was in his dreams and it set off the richly dark brown tones of her body in precisely the same delicious way.

Her dive was just as perfect as everything else about her. she hit the water at precisely the right angle, slicing through it with hardly any splash at all. When she surfaced she saw her brother coming out of the kitchen with the tray of drinks. Then she spotted Prometheus. He was smiling shyly the way he always did around her. In his hands were flowers and candy.

"Hi Helen," he called. "Uh . . . nice day, isn't it?"

She left the pool and quickly went over to a beach chair where she slipped into a long white terrycloth robe. Maximus told her his story about feeling sorry for Prometheus at the steamy playground. Helen seemed to accept it. Prometheus had followed her to the chair but kept some distance between them as he held out his gifts.

"Happy graduation, Helen."

"Thank you," she said softly, taking the roses and sniffing them with delight before putting them down with the chocolates on a glass table beneath a beach umbrella. Then she turned towards the house. "I have a gift for you too, but it's up in my room. I'll get it as soon as I change."

"You're not going to swim anymore?"

"Well, I—"

"Listen sis, interrupted Maximus, "Prometheus came all the way out here for a swim, but I can't stay with him. I just got a call to meet some friends at the Starbucks in Bryn Mawr. Can you drive him home later?"

Helen's eyes sparkled. "Yes, of course."

"Good. I'll leave you two alone then."

She watched her brother depart, then turned to shyly face Prometheus. "It really is kind of hot, isn't it?"

"Uh, yeah," he readily agreed. "It was nice of Maximus to invite me out here to swim."

"You're always welcome here, Prometheus. You always have been."

They stared silently at each other for a moment, then they both looked away for an even longer time. It was Helen who finally spoke again. "Let's go inside. I better get these chocolates out of the heat and the flowers into some water. You can change in the powder room right off the kitchen and get a towel for yourself."

When they came back out they spent most of their time swimming, with little conversation between laps. Helen was an absolutely magnificent swimmer. Of course. She knew all the strokes and did each of them with wonderful form and grace. Prometheus, on the other hand, barely managed to get from one end of the pool to the other with a combination of the crawl and a kind of doggy paddle. He felt embarrassed in front of Helen, but for some strange reason she didn't seem to notice his awkwardness in the water.

After a good hour or more in the pool they stretched out on loungers to sun themselves while they listened to music on a nearby boom-box. Helen told Prometheus how glad she was that he was going to camp. She didn't mention the beauty and goodness she had felt watching him play basketball with Hobie. Shortly after that Helen's mother came out to freshen their drinks, then left them alone once again.

"That was very thoughtful of her," said Prometheus.

Helen smiled. "That's my mom."

"She could have had one of your servants do it."

"*Servants?*" Helen asked.

"Sure. You do have servants, don't you?"

Now Helen laughed. Really laughed. Good and hearty. Fully. Joyfully. Prometheus just loved the musical sound of it, even though he knew that to some extent at least she was actually laughing at him.

"Of course not," she finally managed to blurt out. "Whatever made you think that?"

"Well, who takes care of the house?"

"*We* do, naturally."

"All by yourselves?"

"Yes."

"But it's so big?"

"Not really. Just three bedrooms. Most of the homes around here have five or six. At least."

"I guess you mom has plenty of time to work on the place."

"Guess again."

"She doesn't?"

"Not with her job."

"Your mom . . . works?"

Helen nodded. "Always has."

"What's she do?"

"She's a teacher just like dad, only with much younger children . . . you know, pre-K."

Prometheus pointed at the home. "You may have just three bedrooms, but the place is still really spacious."

"Yeah, and I appreciate that. When I was in grade school mom operated a daycare center out of our apartment. It seemed like there were always kids underfoot just about everywhere you turned when I was growing up."

"She must really like children."

"That she does."

"She's really beautiful too."

"I think so."

Prometheus stared at Helen. Just a bit more boldly than he ever had before. He wanted to say something to her. Something he had wanted to tell her for some time, but never could. Now seemed like the ideal time with her lying there right beside him, but he still had to turn away to get the words out. Even then it was a struggle and he almost choked on them. "Just like her . . . daughter."

"Thank you," Helen whispered, looking utterly surprised and turning her own head away from Prometheus. "Maybe I should take you home now."

"Uh, okay."

He had wanted to do something else, but suddenly it didn't seem to be the right time for that, so he got up and followed Helen back into her house. Without ever holding her hand.

The two of them were pretty quiet again with each other throughout much of the ride back into the city. It was only as they neared Chinatown when Prometheus finally said something again. "This is a nice car you've got, Helen."

"It suits me."

Somehow it did, he realized, although he never suspected her car would turn out to be anything as small as that less than new white Neon. He'd once seen her driving a gold Lexus and had always assumed that was her car. It was only now that he learned it belonged to a friend who had lent it to Helen while the Neon was in the shop.

When Helen left him off in front of the restaurant he had wanted to say something, wanted to do something, but he just stood there waving goodbye and watching her drive away. He still stood there after her car had disappeared from view; thinking about how happy her family had seemed, remembering how his used to be, envying the way he assumed her parents were so proud of both their kids, wondering why he just couldn't seem to bounce back to his old self after his dad's death.

Then he went back to the alley and up the stairs to the apartment, wearing the golden watch Helen had given him as a graduation gift. When he first saw it back at the house and stammered out a question about why . . . she had simply laughed and told him it was because he'd always need to know just what time it really was.

CHAPTER SEVEN

THE CAMP WAS SEVERAL HOURS FROM PHILADELPHIA, HIGH UP IN THE POCONOS near a famous Winter ski resort. It was a sprawling site laid out all along the shore of a beautiful mountain lake. Prometheus was reminded of a place his father had taken them on vacation up in New York state years before. Athena had just gotten her granny glasses around that time and she was wearing them everywhere. Prometheus thought it strange that he should think of that n ow. He didn't know just why he did. Maybe because the camp wasn't all that far from the New York border itself. Or maybe because it was so rare that they had ever before taken a vacation as a family. Or maybe because that was the summer his father first taught him to play basketball.

The camp had plenty of courts. Most of them were already in use as bus after bus arrived to unload new campers. Prometheus thought his bus must have been the very last of them all. He was put in a group assigned to a cabin on the edge of the camp. They had just gotten settled when a paunchy middle-aged Guide showed up and told them they were late for their first session on court #23. They followed him there and were greeted by a tall young woman with a dazzling smile and short blonde hair. She was dressed in the camp's official blue shorts and t-shirt with a red basketball logo on each.

"You guys are really lucky," she said enthusiastically. "For some strange reason your group's one of the very few this summer that gets to personally train with our best junior instructor . . . a man who's been a real all-star in local college basketball these past two seasons."

"Who's that?" Prometheus asked.

The answer came from behind him. First the sound of a ball being dribbled so hard that it seemed to thunder. Then the laugh. The horrible arrogant grating laugh. He knew who it was before he turned around.

"Hi, Jap," Durk whispered as he passed by on his way to stand beside the woman in the middle of the circle.

Everyone started applauding when they realized just who their instructor was going to be. Durk smiled and bowed as he graciously acknowledged their applause. Then his face grew serious as he held the ball out in front of him at about shoulder height.

"Fellas, let's get right down to business. The first lesson, the most important lesson, you've got to learn in basketball is that you've always got to—"

Without any warning he suddenly shot the ball into Prometheus' gut with such force that it knocked him down. Just like he'd done before at the playground.

"*—stay on your feet!*"

Prometheus heard the sound of people laughing. Just like he'd heard it before. It sure was going to be a great summer. Hobie had insisted that he'd learn a lot.

*　　*　　*

Actually, of course, it *did* turn out to be a great summer.

Strange in the extreme, but still great. Even in the beginning, which was the worst part. And Prometheus really did learn a lot. A hell of a lot. Not all of it stuff that he had any desire to learn, and some of it things he would have absolutely preferred not to learn, but still in all he learned.

One of the most important things he learned in those first few days was how to avoid Durk. That wasn't easy. He was their chief instructor, but he wasn't their only instructor. Whenever possible Prometheus would switch to another class at the time Durk was teaching his. Not that it always worked, but the fact that it worked at all was enough to give him a little peace. The strange thing was that Durk came looking for him. He didn't know why. Durk treated Prometheus just like he always did at the playground, except for one thing. At camp he whispered all his racist cracks so that Prometheus was the only one to hear him. Prometheus supposed camp was better. But not much.

The first week was a mixed affair. Prometheus had fun swimming in the lake and actually learned some real strokes like the breast and back-stroke. He got berated and humiliated by Durk in front of everyone on the basketball courts. Constantly. He thoroughly enjoyed some great biking on mysterious pathways that wandered through the dense woods surrounding the camp. He thoroughly hated the weight room. He'd loved it in high school, especially those old Nautilus machines. But at camp Durk was always there, always adding more and more weights, always leading the laughter when Prometheus could no longer move the bar. Singing at the nightly campfire was heaven. Playing daily basketball games was hell. Not that he got to really *play* all that much. Durk continually substituted players throughout every game, but he'd never send Prometheus in until maybe the last minute or so, and only if the score was so lopsided that it couldn't possible affect the outcome of the game either way. There was little point in protesting such treatment. Durk seemed to be the boss of his own domain. None of the adults around seemed willing to contradict anything he did.

The second week was a repeat of the first. With one important and wonderful exception. It began on a Friday afternoon. Prometheus was out jogging on the main road several miles from camp. Helen came biking along from the opposite direction. She looked so incredibly beautiful. So fresh in her music camp's dazzling white shorts and T-shirt. So sweet when she smiled after spotting him. Back at her house they'd both been too shy to actually have arranged to meet in the mountains.

They talked for a long time there on the side of the road. She pointed out across the lake to show him where her camp was located. Then she told him about the dance they were having the next night. He said that was nice. Then she invited him to come to the dance . . . as her guest. He couldn't believe it. Him? Helen? But he thought how he wasn't stupid. At least not all the time. He didn't give her a chance to reconsider. He said he'd be there and he pointed to the gold watch she'd given him, saying that he'd be on time.

Durk didn't bother him the rest of that day or the next. Not that Durk didn't try. He just didn't succeed.

*   *   *

Prometheus had a little trouble finding the camp, but none in finding the dance once he got there. Music was blaring from an open-sided pavilion that extended right out over the waters of the lake, There were tiny plastic Japanese lanterns of different colors marking the path down to the pavilion. Helen was waiting for him there on the path. She was lovelier than he had ever seen her before. Her huge eyes sparkled. Everything about her sparkled. The light from the full moon looked gorgeous on the lake, but it looked better shining on her hair. The short pale pink dress she wore didn't show as much of her deliciously dark brown legs as did her white short shorts the day before, but it still showed enough to make him happy.

Helen took his hand as they walked down to the pavilion. There were plenty of other couples all around them but he hardly noticed them. He never thought of himself as much of a dancer but with Helen in his arms he thought he moved like a master. The music just seemed to carry them along like a gently flowing stream. She asked him about camp, then laughed at his reply.

"So *that's* your deeply considered evaluation of the whole place?"

"Yes," he answered firmly.

" . . . 'half-and-half'?"

"Precisely."

She laughed again. "Precisely meaning what?"

"Meaning that half the time I love it and the other half I can't stand it!"

"Let me guess," she said, "the half you love is whenever you're playing basketball, right?"

"Well . . . no, it's actually just the—"

He was distracted by the chilling sight of Durk entering the pavilion with a bunch of his friends. They were all being greeted enthusiastically by lots of other people on the dance floor.

"Actually it's just *what?*" asked Helen.

"Oh . . . uh, never mind. How do you like your camp?"

"I just love it! No 'half-and-half' either. I'm talking about pure, unadulterated, absolutely total love!"

Durk spotted Prometheus and headed straight for him.

"Uh . . . that's nice," Prometheus said. "Why don't we go outside and—"

He tried guiding her off the dance floor, but it was too late. Durk stepped between them and eyed Helen with a look of total lust.

"Well, well, well . . . " he drawled. "What have we here . . . 'Beauty and the Beast' . . . or just the Fox and the Jap?"

"We were just leaving," said Prometheus.

"So *leave* already! The babe and I have some serious dancin' to do."

Durk grabbed Helen by the waist and pulled her away from Prometheus. It was in that very instant that Prometheus moved. He didn't think about it. He didn't hesitate. He just hauled off and punched Durk squarely in the jaw with a roundhouse-right. Durk dropped to his knees. Not exactly knocked out, but definitely stunned and hurting. He rubbed his jaw, then he shook his head to clear it. He looked up at Prometheus in sheer amazement.

"You . . . hit me . . . first."

Prometheus stared at his own fist. It tingled just a bit, but didn't really hurt. He was surprised at how easy it had been and he wondered just why that was so. When Durk had slapped him on the playground he had been totally unable to return the blow. Durk had blocked him then so effortlessly. Now he looked down at Durk who somehow seemed to be finding the whole thing totally unbelievable as he stared up at Helen.

"He hit me . . . *first.*"

Helen shook her head. "Well, you really were acting rather obnoxiously, you know, so I think Prometheus had every—"

"*First,*" he repeated, ignoring Helen now and starting to grin broadly. "Prometheus actually hit me *first!*"

Durk stood up, still rubbing his jaw, but not looking at all like he wanted to fight. The strange thing was that he actually looked kind of happy. Prometheus turned around and slowly walked out of the pavilion. Durk didn't follow him. Prometheus heard him laughing, but the really strange thing was that it was nothing like his usual kind of laughter. It wasn't a mean or taunting laugh. It wasn't a put-down laugh. It wasn't a laugh of derision. It was something much more strange. It was somehow more a laugh of relief.

Prometheus made his way back up the path of the Japanese lanterns, crossed the wide parking lot, and started down a narrow dirt trail that led off into the woods. It was then that he saw someone walking towards him. It was a dark figure. A strange dark figure with a suitcase in one hand and a blue basketball in the other.

"Hobie?!" Prometheus shouted as he ran to close the distance between them, "what are you doing here?"

"Got me a job," the old man answered.

"Where?"

"Right here at the music camp."

"Doing what?"

"Oh, general janitorial duties and the like. I'm good at that."

"But why?"

"Why? Cause I've had lots of practice, that's why."

"No, no," said Prometheus. "I mean why work at all?"

"Oh . . . that. Well, the vacation got kind of boring. They usually do after a week or so."

"But why did you take a job all the way up here?"

Hobie grinned. "I guess I just wanted to keep closer tabs on my 'investment'. You glad to see me?"

"Of course," Prometheus began. "It's only that—"

Hobie fired the ball straight at his face. Fast. Hard. Prometheus caught it with ease. They walked together over towards a huge trash compactor near a shed at the very edge of the woods.

"So how you doin', boy?"

"I . . . don't know."

"What the hell is that supposed to mean?"

"I just punched a guy."

"Who?"

"Durk."

Hobie threw back his head and laughed long and loudly. "Hell, that boy's had it coming for quite a while now."

"Yeah," Prometheus agreed. "He's been on my case ever since I got to camp. Ever since I was in junior high, in fact . . . but still, I don't know if I should have hit him first."

Hobie froze in his tracks and stopped laughing. He grabbed Prometheus by both arms and shook him.

"You hit him *first?*"

"Yeah."

"That's not good, Prometheus, not good at all."

"Why?"

"There's danger in that boy."

Now it was Prometheus who laughed. He shook his head. "Nah, for all his size and strength he didn't even try to hit me back. I was kind of surprised at that."

"I'm not," said Hobie. "You just beware of him."

"You think he'll try to get me?"

"He will," Hobie said solemnly.

"I'm not afraid of him."

Hobie pointed a stubby little finger at him. "You *better* be afraid, boy . . . you damn well better be!"

"Why, because he's bigger?"

"No, because he's the opposite of you."

"What do you mean?"

"You figure it out."

Prometheus thought for a second. "Oh, you mean because he's such a racist and all?"

"Racist?" Hobie asked, looking strangely at Prometheus. "You think he's a racist?"

"Well . . . sure."

"Why?"

"Because of the way he talks . . . and acts."

"And that's what makes you think he's a racist?"

"Yeah. Don't you think so?"

Hobie shook his head. "Not particularly."

"But he's always—"

"Listen boy, human beings are the most peculiar kind of creatures in existence. What they say and even what they do ain't always connected to what they really are inside. They're so damn hard to figure out that it must give the gods themselves some powerful headaches."

"What's that got to do with Durk?"

"Well, you're the one judgin' him to be a racist by his words and actions towards you, right?"

"Of course."

"So by the same token you probably figure that say . . . all slave-holders in the old south were racists too, huh?"

"They were!"

Again the old man shook his head. "Not all of them."

"Aw, come on, Hobie. How could anyone own slaves and not be a racist. That doesn't make any sense!"

"Sure it does."

"How?"

"Simple. Some of them folks didn't connect bein' a slave with bein' any particular race. They would've been equally willin' to have white slaves or Indian or whatever they could've gotten."

Prometheus looked dumbfounded. "Well . . . even if that was true they were still racists because they thought blacks were inferior and deserved to be slaves."

"Not all of them thought that."

"How can you—"

"Some of them knew that black people were just as human as they were. The trouble was that that didn't make any difference to them. Just like it didn't make any difference to the Africans and Arabs who took part in the slave trade. They didn't give a damn either way whether you were their equal or not. All they cared about was that you could be their slave."

Hobie laughed as he watched Prometheus holding his head in his hands. "What's the matter, boy?"

"You're making my head spin . . . literally."

"Good. People need to have their heads spun now and again. It makes them think for themselves for a change."

"But Hobie, what you're telling me—"

"Let me make it spin some more. Not all slavers were racists, but I suppose you think that *none* of say . . . the Abolitionists were either, right?"

"I suppose."

"Wrong! In some cases it was just the opposite side of that strange coin of human irrationality and evil. Just like there were some folks who knew black people were in no way inferior to them, yet were still willing to have them as slaves . . . there were other people who fought to free the slaves because they sincerely thought slavery to be an evil institution in itself, yet still considered blacks to be less than human."

"In other words," mumbled Prometheus, "you're trying to tell me that—"

"Some people who favored slavery weren't racists, and some who opposed it were!"

"But where's Durk fit in? I still think he's a racist. I just can't see even the tiniest bit of good in him."

Hobie's huge blue eye shone brightly in the moonlight as he stared with an almost angry intensity at Prometheus. "Boy, who the hell said anything about 'good'."

"Well, if he's not a racist—"

"He's something worse," snapped Hobie, "something far far worse."

"What?"

Hobie didn't answer. The discussion was finished. He had just spotted an empty peach basket in the trash and went over to pull it out. Then he took it over to a tall tree, punched out the bottom of the basket, and motioned for Prometheus to bend over. He climbed up on the younger man's shoulders and attached the basket to the tree by twisting some of its wire around a broken branch. Then he pointed at his creation and grinned.

"This is how it all began . . . at least in its latest reincarnation."

"Yeah," said Prometheus. "I heard that story too. I wonder if it's really true."

"It is."

"How do you know?"

"Simple," Hobie replied with a chuckle. "I was there at the time."

They played basketball. Despite the camp, or maybe *because* of it, thought Prometheus, he felt a little rusty at first, but it didn't take long before he started regaining some of the magic he had been developing back in the city.

Soon he was moving more quickly and smoothly than ever, in perfect harmony with Hobie.

"Did you ever teach anyone else," Prometheus asked his teacher, "besides me?"

Hobie snickered. "Oh . . . one or two."

"Who?"

The old man named a player.

"Never heard of him."

"Then you don't know basketball."

"When did he play?"

"Oh . . . late eighties or so."

Prometheus laughed. "What . . . the *eighteen*-eighties?"

"Yes."

"How bout someone from *this* century?"

Hobie named another player.

"Never heard of him either. When was this one active?"

"Early twenties. Al Capone used to like his style."

And so it went. They kept playing the most fantastic game of one-on-one they'd ever had, and Hobie kept naming players from the turn-of-the century up until about World War II, and Prometheus kept repeating that he'd never heard of any of them. When he asked if the players were even famous in their own time, Hobie admitted that they were not. He insisted that they were something much more important than famous. They were *good*.

Prometheus went in for a quick lay-up. "Did you ever teach anyone who was both good *and* famous?"

Hobie dropped a final name. Prometheus dropped the ball.

"You've got to be kidding!"

"Not about him," said Hobie . . . "especially not about him."

"Then that's the *real* reason he's called Magic?"

"You got it, boy."

Prometheus may have gotten that, but suddenly he didn't have much luck getting the ball. When he reached back for it Hobie blurred past him and sank a fast shot. When Prometheus tried going after him, he tripped over his own feet. With good reason. He saw Helen watching him. She stood in the shadows of another tree, looking like she'd been hypnotized. Prometheus stopped playing. Then Hobie saw her too and went over to her.

"What did you see, girl?"

"I . . . I don't know," she stammered, a wide-eyed look of wonder filling her face. "It was so beautiful . . . like chamber music or something."

Hobie nodded. "That's because there's only two of us playing. When there's ten, it's like a symphony."

"It's also kind of like a ballet."

That made Hobie clap his hands. "Yes, yes," he shouted. "You see that, do you?"

"I think so."

And do you like to dance yourself, Helen?"

"Oh yes!"

"Were you and Prometheus dancing together tonight?"

"A little," she began, "but then—"

"How was he?"

"Terrible," Prometheus interjected firmly.

Helen shook her head. "I wouldn't say that. He was actually rather"

"You could make him better," offered Hobie.

"I'm not a dance teacher," she said.

"Of course you are, Helen. "Just like I am, but I've already taught the boy most of what I know."

Prometheus smirked at such strange talk. "Hobie, you haven't been teaching me any dancing at all. You've been teaching me basketball, remember?"

"Same thing," said Hobie, waving his hand in dismissal at such a meaningless distinction.

"Are you going to play some more?" Helen asked.

"Yes," said Hobie.

"No," Prometheus countered.

Hobie looked shocked. "Why the hell not?"

"I don't like people watching."

"Damn it!" Hobie shouted. "You damn well better *start* liking it. The whole purpose of basketball is to bring joy and truth and beauty and hope to this world and its people. Helen here is one of those people . . . a very special one, if I'm not mistaken, and I never am! She seems attuned to the essence of the game to a degree that all you people should be, but so very few of you ever are. The girl has insight! You better learn to respect that."

"Okay, okay," said Prometheus. "maybe you're right."

Hobie's eye had been burning into his with an intensity Prometheus hadn't seen or felt before. He turned away from the old man to tell Helen she could watch after all.

She was gone.

CHAPTER EIGHT

SOMEHOW PROMETHEUS MANAGED TO AVOID DURK ALL DAY SUNDAY. THAT only delayed the inevitable, of course, and sure enough it was still early Monday morning when Durk spotted him crossing the far end of the gym on his way to the weight room.

"Hey, Prometheus!"

That was strange. He called him by his real name. Not Jap or Gook or Slope or Yella Nigger, like he used to back on the playground. Not Shorty or Wimp or Stupid or just *You*! like he'd been doing at camp. He actually called him Prometheus.

"Hey, Prometheus . . . c'mon down here for a minute, will you?"

Durk had been working under the net with two guys who made even him look short. Prometheus figured one of them must have been a true seven-footer. The other one wasn't far from it. Durk was smiling and waving eagerly for Prometheus to join them. It was strange how that smile wasn't at all like his usual one. There was actually some warmth in it. Like a *real* smile. Like he was honestly glad to see Prometheus.

"Here you go, killer . . . " Durk said, lightly tossing the ball to Prometheus. "Let's show these clowns the way rebounding's supposed to be done."

Prometheus started slowly dribbling the ball towards the basket. Suddenly the two giants made a break at him and he was forced to move faster. A lot faster. They still would have been all over him in another instant if Durk hadn't jumped into action along his side, taking a quick pass from him and leading them away. Prometheus returned the favor and soon they had a real rhythm going between them. They were the first to score and that set a pattern for the next ten minutes. Their opponents not only had about a six inch height advantage on Durk and nearly a foot on Prometheus, but they were both powerfully built guys who knew how to use both their bulk and their strength to their benefit. In addition, they looked as old or older than Durk. They were either college players like him or in their sixth or seventh year of high school.

In any case it did them little good. Durk and Prometheus consistently out-maneuvered and out-shot them. As the game went on Prometheus started returning Durk's ready smile. They were proud of themselves. After the last basket the big guys left, but Durk kept Prometheus out on the court giving him pointers on how to fake out an opponent. It was stuff Prometheus had never known before. He learned a lot from Durk that day.

*   *   *

That night he told Hobie all about it. They were playing a rather leisurely game together at the music camp, moving all around very lightly and grace-fully, only occasionally bothering to toss Hobie's mysterious blue sphere into the peach basket.

"He was real friendly," Prometheus said. "I never saw him like that before in my life. I can't believe it."

"I can," said Hobie with a frown.

"It's so strange. He never used to be at all interested in how I played. He always ignored me. Totally. But now it's like he really wants to help. Like he wants to show me stuff."

"That he does."

"But why? It just doesn't make any sense. I can't see that anything's changed between the two of us . . . other than the fact that I hit him."

Prometheus laughed. Hobie looked at him gravely. "You did more than that."

"What?"

"You hit him *first*."

"Why the hell would that make him want to teach me anything?"

"It's simple," said Hobie. "He wants to teach you to *keep on* hitting first."

"What do you mean?"

The old man's eye narrowed its gaze on Prometheus. "Tell me something, boy, do you believe in vampires?"

"Vampires? No, of course not."

"You should."

"What . . . are you kidding? Do *you* believe in them?"

"Absolutely."

"Aw, come on, Hobie, how can you—"

"I ain't talkin' bout the kind that suck away your blood. Those are just a myth, but like all myths there's more than a grain of truth there."

"What truth?"

"The truth that there's creatures out there who will suck away your *spirit* . . . your soul . . . your own self, the force you have in you for the good."

"Why would they want to do that?"

Hobie frowned. "Because just like the mythical vampires they want to make you into something like themselves."

*   *   *

The next afternoon Durk used Prometheus to demonstrate rebounding to several different classes. He smiled at everything Prometheus did, and even clapped a couple of times. After the last class had been dismissed he kept Prometheus out on the court again for some personal instruction. This time the subject was how to foul an opponent without being called on it. He made it seem like fun. Prometheus was laughing so much he finally had to put up his hands for Durk to stop.

"What's wrong, Prometheus?"

"Well, this is really great stuff and all. Only aren't these moves kind of . . . well . . . illegal?"

"No," Durk replied, laughing that great laugh of his that Prometheus was really starting to like. "Illegal is when you get *caught* doing them. You do things my way and you won't get caught."

"I see . . . "

Durk's smile vanished. "I hope you do."

*   *   *

That night at the music camp Prometheus was waiting for Hobie to finish his job. To kill the time he started warming up by dancing to some fast hip-hop on the boom-box he had brought along. When Hobie finally appeared he promptly went right over to the machine and hit the stop button.

"What was that you were doin' just now?" he demanded of Prometheus.

"Dancing."

"No it weren't either."

"Oh yeah . . . well, what was it then?"

"The opposite of dancing," Hobie replied firmly.

"Why's that?"

"Cause it's got no grace, no beauty, no strength . . . and most especially no life or soul. Does that answer your question?"

"Yeah, but—"

"What were you playin'?"

"Oh, it's the very latest in Gangsta Rap . . . so new it's not even officially released yet."

"Then where did you get it?"

"From Durk."

"I see . . ."

"What do you think of it?"

"I think it's foul."

Prometheus was annoyed. "Hey, do you even know what Gangsta Rappers are?"

"Sure I do, boy. They're a bunch of Stepin Fetchits tommin' for the worst kind of white folks. Kind of reminds me of the old Minstrel shows."

"But listen, Hobie, you got to admit that maybe apart from my style of dancing to it, the music itself does have soul . . . and lots of it."

"Not *human* soul."

"Yeah . . . well, what kind of music do you think has 'human' soul to it . . . Bach and Beethoven and that kind of stuff?"

Hobie nodded gravely. "Without a shadow of a doubt."

"You can have it. I'm just not into things like that."

Now Hobie closed his eye briefly as he shook his head. "If you spend enough time with Helen maybe you will be, but in the meantime maybe I can give you something to help."

"I don't need any help," Prometheus insisted.

"You surely do, boy."

With that Hobie led him down a narrow overgrown path through the woods that led to the tiny cabin where he lived. Inside Prometheus noticed a boom-box several times the size of his own. It was surrounded by high stacks of CDs which also littered the table and the bed. Hobie went right to work picking and choosing one record after the other which he handed to Prometheus. Some of the artists Prometheus knew. Many he did not. Louis Armstrong. Sidney Bechet. Bix. Diz. Prez. Bird. Monk. Mingus. Miles. Duke Ellington. Billie Holiday. Count Basie. Sarah Vaughan. Dave Brubeck. Sonny Rollins. Stan Getz. Ella Fitzgerald. Bill Evans. George Russell. Jimmy Knepper. Jelly Roll Morton. Jim Hall. John Coltrane.

"These are all jazz," said Prometheus.

Hobie grinned. "That's *one* name for it."

Prometheus held the stack of discs against his chest with both hands. "What am I supposed to do with all this?"

"*Listen* to it, of course!"

"When?"

"Whenever you got the time . . . and I suggest you either find or make that time every day."

Hobie put the CDs into a paper bag and motioned for Prometheus to follow him back outside. "Now let's make some of our own music."

*   *   *

Back under the make-shift basket Hobie took a Duke Ellington record from the bag and put it on Prometheus' boom-box. He then tossed him the ball as the song "Things Ain't What They Used To Be" began.

After the first few measures of the song Prometheus and Hobie were soon playing harder and faster than they ever had before. Prometheus wasn't getting anywhere with the old man so he decided to try one of the new moves Durk had taught him. It worked! Hobie went down hard and Prometheus made a spectacular basket. When he helped his teacher up he noticed he wasn't smiling like Durk had.

"Where the hell you'd learn that?"

"From Durk."

"That figures."

"What do you think of it?"

"I think it stinks."

"Why?"

"It's a foul. You know that."

"Yeah, I suppose . . . but I don't think it would be called."

Hobie's eyes narrowed on him. "What the hell does *that* have to do with anything?"

"Uh . . . maybe . . . just everything," suggested Prometheus.

"Uh . . . maybe . . . just nothing," Hobie countered, mocking his tone. The Ellington orchestra played on.

*   *   *

It seemed to Prometheus that he was really learning now. On Wednesday he and Durk were challenged to a rematch with the giants. It was cut-throat two-on-two with beers as the stakes. There was no contest. The giants didn't have a chance. Durk said he thought Prometheus had payed at his most aggressive level yet. Throughout the game Prometheus had followed Durk's lead and constantly faked out their competition. When that didn't work he just plain cheated. Durk laughed at that.

"You're a natural, kid," he said.

*   *   *

The moonlight still looked great on the lake by the music camp, but Prometheus thought it strange that Helen never seemed to be around when he came to practice. Hobie was always there, of course, but there were times when Prometheus wished he wasn't. Like the second time he tried one of the great tricks he'd learnt from Durk. In the gym it had enabled him to actually floor one of the giants. At the music camp things went a little differently.

Several times Hobie had managed to twist out of the way just in time when Prometheus tried to put a move on him, but then he suddenly stood his ground and the two of them made contact. Hard contact. Strangely though, Prometheus was the one who got floored. He looked up at the old man. Astonished. Hobie looked angry.

"What the hell were you doin', boy?"

"Playing basketball."

"No sir," Hobie insisted as he helped him up, "that sure weren't no basketball you was playin' just then. No way."

"What was it then?"

"It was *Durk*."

"Aw, Hobie, he's not all that bad."

Hobie nodded. "All that and so very much more."

"You just don't know him," Prometheus protested. "Not like I do."

"That's right, son . . . not like you do."

"He's helping me."

"How?"

"By showing me stuff . . . the kind of stuff you never show me . . . stuff that's making me a better player."

Hobie snickered. "You think you're gettin' *better*?"

"I *know* I am."

The old man shook his head and smiled sadly. Then he led Prometheus out to a spot further away from the peach basket and handed him the ball. "Shoot," he whispered.

"And just what are *you* going to be doing?" Prometheus asked suspiciously.

"Just shoot."

Prometheus took careful aim, checked to make sure Hobie wasn't trying anything, then took his shot. The ball bounced off the rim. Close, but no basket.

"Again."

"It's you," Prometheus argued. "You're making me nervous."

"Again."

Hobie turned his back, closed his eyes, and put his hands in his pockets. Prometheus dribbled the ball several times, took even more careful aim than before, and then shot. This time the ball even missed the rim. Hobie turned back around to face him.

"Again."

In frustration Prometheus recovered the ball and shot it again without any real preparation. It hit the rim and rode around it a few times before dropping off again. Hobie then snatched up the ball and took it back even further from the basket than where they had been before.

"Again."

"Aw man, this is even more than a regular three-pointer."

"Again."

Prometheus shot and missed badly. "It's just too long a shot."

"You've made longer," Hobie said, "*before* you came up here."

"And I can make them again!"

Hobie ran to the basket, got the ball, and took it out to regular foul-shooting distance. "Show me."

Prometheus tried. It was his worst shot yet. "Sinking long shots isn't everything," he said.

"I know that, son."

"There's a lot more to playing basketball than just that."

"Absolutely."

Prometheus wanted to cry. He would have cried, but what he wanted even more was that Hobie not see him doing so. Still, he supposed his voice probably sounded choked up when he spoke to the old man. "Hobie, what's wrong with me? Everything is so strange. During the day I really think I'm getting better, but then I come over here at night and I can't do anything. It's different somehow here with you then it is with Durk. Why did you ever want me to come up here?"

"To learn."

"But it seems like—"

"Learnin' ain't always easy, boy, not *real* learnin'. Sometimes it's painful and sometimes it's downright dangerous. That's when you learn the most . . . when you've got the most to lose."

"But do you think I even am . . . learning, that is?"

"That remains to be seen."

Hobie put his arm around him. It was the first time he'd ever done that. Then he retrieved the ball and handed it to his pupil. Its deep blue colors were glowing more than ever in the pale moon-light.

"Keep this."

Prometheus looked at the ball in his hands. It felt kind of warm now, almost alive even. Then he looked at Hobie and shook his head. "Oh no, I mean . . . thanks, thanks a lot, really . . . but I just couldn't. This is your—"

"I ain't talkin' bout *forever!*" Hobie snapped.

"Oh . . . what then?"

"Just till you *really* start gettin' better. Keep it with you all the time, even when you're not playin'. Do you understand me, boy?"

"Well, uh . . . no, not really. I—"

"Just do it!"

"Okay," said Prometheus, trying to spin the ball on his index finger. "Same time tomorrow night?"

"No. You might just be playin' a little too much lately. Take a break this weekend, but don't forget what I just told you about the ball."

*   *   *

Like most practices on Fridays, the next morning included a full game. Prometheus' team was dominating their opposition all through some really rough play. Durk was the referee. He called no fouls.

The game ended and everyone headed for the locker room, but then Prometheus stopped as he remembered to go back to one of the first row bleachers where he'd left the blue ball wrapped in a beach towel. He was just picking it up when Durk approached from behind him.

"What's that?" he asked.

"My good-luck charm."

"Let's see it."

Prometheus pulled off the towel and held the ball up to him. There was no glow to it in the daylight, but Prometheus thought it still must have looked kind of strange the first time one saw it. Even so, Durk's reaction was even stranger. He took one quick glance at it, went wide-eyed and started wiping sweat off his face, even though Prometheus didn't see any there. Then without another word Durk suddenly turned and ran away.

*   *   *

Late that afternoon Prometheus was walking down the road leading from camp to the town. It was a distance of several miles, but he'd missed the last bus and figured the exercise wouldn't hurt. The blue ball was under his arm, but occasionally he'd dribble it along the asphalt. The road had been deserted for quite some time, but just then he heard a car coming up fast behind him. From the sound it had a really powerful engine. He stepped over into the grass just before it rounded the bend and went roaring past him. It was a Mercedes, a brand new bright red Mercedes.

Its brakes squealed as it slammed to a sudden stop right up ahead just before another bend in the winding road. Then it backed up towards Prometheus and the front passenger door opened. He put the ball back under his arm and ran up to the car. He figured it might be someone from the camp offering him a ride into town. He wasn't wrong. It was Durk.

"Goin' to town, young man?"

"Yes, sir."

"Hop in then."

He didn't have to make the offer twice. What a car, thought Prometheus. The interior was a deeply plush black velvet. Punk Rock blasted from speakers that seemed to be everywhere. He had just sat down when Durk threw the shift into gear and the car accelerated from zero to what felt at least ninety in about two seconds flat. Prometheus was thrown back into his seat. The ball sailed over into Durk's lap. He panicked.

"Get it away! Get it away!"

"Okay," Prometheus said, lifting it off him. "What's the matter? Strange as it may appear, this thing is really just a basketball. That's all."

Durk was breathing very heavily. Prometheus noticed that as he started calming down he also started to become rather embarrassed.

"Uh . . . yeah, just a ball, sure . . . but it could be dangerous. It could interfere with my driving, you know . . . uh, jam up under a pedal or something."

"Yeah, I suppose it could. Thanks for picking me up."

"My pleasure," said Durk, obviously relieved to be off the subject of the ball. "In fact, thanks for everything lately."

Durk turned down the music. "What do you mean?"

"You know . . . teaching me, showing me all that great new stuff and all."

"That's my job."

"Yeah, but you've been giving me lots of individual attention, lots of extra time . . . more than you do with the other guys."

Durk grinned. "Maybe that's because I just happen to think you've got more potential than they do."

He had to slow down because they were nearing the outskirts of the town. Prometheus wanted to tell him something. He had wanted to tell him for days, but it was proving more difficult than he had thought it would be. He knew he better do it soon because it wouldn't be long before he'd be getting out of the car and somehow that seemed just the right place to do it.

"Listen, Durk . . . I'm sorry I hit you that night."

Durk laughed. "Forget it."

"I shouldn't have done it. I don't know what got into me."

"Don't worry about it. I was so drunk I probably had it coming."

Prometheus though that was strange, but then again maybe Durk was just trying to be nice. To be gracious in accepting his apology. To make it easy for him. Yeah, that had to be it. He really was one hell of a guy after all. Prometheus was learning more and more every day. The strange thing was than he just didn't remember Durk having been drunk at all the night of the dance. He had seemed just as cold sober then as he always did.

"That doesn't matter, Durk. I don't go around hitting people . . . especially not hitting them *first*. I never do that."

"Maybe you should."

"Huh?"

"You know something, Prometheus, I'm sorry too about something. Real sorry."

"What?"

"The way I used to pick on you and tease you and all. I never really meant most of it that much."

"Then why'd you do it?" Prometheus asked.

Durk looked more seriously at Prometheus. "It might have been because me and my folks were always so poor. Guess I was kind of jealous of your family owning the restaurant and all."

"Jealous?" asked Prometheus, grinning and pointing at the car. "We could never afford anything like this . . . or even close to it."

Durk laughed with him. "My boy, there are ways of getting around poverty."

"Oh yeah? I'd sure like to learn them."

"You will," said Durk.

*   *   *

They were entering the town proper then. It was much more crowded than it ever was during the week. Kids from all the camps in the area were milling about the streets looking for some action. Durk stopped at a traffic light about a block from the bus station in the exact center of town. That's where he was going to park. Prometheus carefully watched the restless crowds of campers, hoping to catch sight of Helen, but not having any luck. He hadn't seen her since the night of the dance. The night he hit Durk. First.

"You weren't jealous," Prometheus said. ""You couldn't have been. Not of me. What was the real reason you were always on my case?"

Durk shrugged. "I don't know . . . not really. Maybe I thought you were kind of a stuck-up little goody-goody."

"Me?"

"And kind of strange."

"*Me?*"

They both laughed together. "So I was wrong," said Durk.

"I hope so."

"Yeah, Prometheus, I really was. It's been nice to find out that you're human after all, just like the rest of us."

The light changed and they drove down the last block to the bus station. Durk eased the Mercedes into the parking lot there and was lucky to find a spot not too far from the entrance. They both got out.

"Thanks again for the ride," said Prometheus.

Durk put a hand on his shoulder. "What are you going to do here in town?"

"I don't know. Maybe see a movie."

"That doesn't sound like much fun all by yourself."

"Guess not," Prometheus admitted, "but it beats staying all alone in camp."

"Why don't you hang with me and my gang?"

"Really?"

"Sure. We're gonna go clubbing. You'll like everybody. Just put that damn thing in the trunk," Durk said, motioning towards the blue ball.

Prometheus took it around to the back of the car where Durk popped the trunk latch. Once the ball was safely inside he came up behind Prometheus and slammed the trunk closed with tremendous force.

"You're really going to have a great time tonight," said Durk, turning around and leading the way to the bus terminal.

CHAPTER NINE

TEN MINUTES LATER THEY WERE MEETING AN INCOMING BUS. SEVERAL ELDERLY passengers got off first. They were followed by two women. The smaller of the pair was carrying a suitcase. They were the two most erotic looking women Prometheus had ever even imagined, let alone seen in the flesh. They appeared so fantastic that somehow they didn't seem quite real. It was as if they couldn't actually exist on the same earth as Prometheus. They both ran to Durk and hugged him with great enthusiasm. He made the introductions.

"Prometheus, this is my fiancee . . . Pandora De Fay."

She was extremely tall and voluptuous with long silky blonde hair.

"And her room mate . . . Eris Yin."

Prometheus saw Eris as a goddess. An incredibly erotic Eurasian goddess. A sensuously seductive goddess who put mere mortal women to shame. Her short thin bright red cocktail dress seemed molded to all the wonderful curves of her small sexy compact body, as her black fishnet stockings clung tightly to her extraordinarily shapely legs. Her dark green eyes were as piercing as the smoky scent that seemed to surround her. She smiled enchantingly as she extended a delicately bejewelled hand to be kissed. Prometheus obeyed without hesitation.

"Ladies," said Durk, "this is Prometheus Go. He's going to turn out to be the new super-star at camp this year."

Though Prometheus wouldn't have thought it possible, the fire in Eris' eyes actually seemed to intensify. She reached out and lightly ran one of her long nails along his naked forearm.

"Prometheus . . . " she practically purred, "that's an unusual name. Are you Greek?"

"Yes," he answered. Anything. Anything you want me to be.

"Oh really? You look about as Greek as I do," she whispered sweetly in his face.

"Half-Greek," he quickly added.

"What's your other half?"

"Japanese."

"Mmmm . . . interesting combination. I like it."

Durk looked all around the station. "Where's your boyfriend?"

Eris was busy staring intently at Prometheus and smiling. It seemed to him that she turned to answer Durk only with the greatest reluctance. "Oh . . . you mean Epi? He injured himself at practice this afternoon."

"Seriously?" asked Durk.

"No. The team doctors say he'll probably be out of the hospital in less than a week."

"But you came anyway?"

"I figured I had nothing better to do," she said, turning her attention back to Prometheus again. "I'm glad now that I didn't."

She took him by the arm as they all left the station and headed back to Durk's car. Prometheus thought how Durk had really been a prophet. He definitely was going to have a great time that night.

*　　*　　*

It certainly started out that way. Dinner confirmed it.

They drove to an elegant French restaurant on the other side of town where Prometheus had the finest food and wine he'd ever experienced. Not to mention the most expensive. Strangely there were no prices listed on the menu and he'd recklessly offered to pay for both himself and Eris. Luckily Durk wouldn't hear of it. He insisted that the whole night be on him. He'd just added another credit card to his collection and he said he was anxious to break it in properly. Prometheus was thankful when he finally saw the bill. He didn't possess even a single credit card, and his cash on hand wouldn't have been enough for a decent tip.

After dinner they started on the night clubs. At the very first one Prometheus thought he'd hit a real snag, but Durk came through as usual and took care of everything just like he did at the restaurant, just like he was starting to do with more and more things in Prometheus' life.

The problem was age. They had handed the Mercedes over to a parking attendant and were all laughing and talking loudly as they made their way up to the front door of the club. The tall doorman there readily admitted Durk, Pandora, and Eris, but he put out a large white-gloved hand to bar the way of Prometheus.

"What's wrong?" asked Durk.

"Nothing, sir. I'd just like to see some I.D. on this particular young person."

"I think he left it back at camp."

The doorman lowered his hand and smiled. In an instant his whole attitude had become immeasurably more friendly. "Oh, is he one of *your* boys, Durk?"

Durk shook his head. "No."

"Then I'm awfully sorry," said the doorman, a truly pained look on his face, "but I'm afraid I'll have to—"

"He's one of my *men*," said Durk.

That did it. The doorman looked relieved. "Is that true?" he asked Prometheus. "Are you one of Durk's?"

"Totally," replied Prometheus.

The nightclub was noisy, smoky, and incredibly crowded. As the night went on it got noisier, smokier, and even more crowded. Pandora danced with Durk. Prometheus danced with Eris. Only it wasn't really dancing, he realized. It was something else. She clung to him. She molded her lush luscious body to his. She held him so tightly he could hardly breathe, could hardly move. They stayed in the same spot throughout whole tunes. Regardless of tempo.

"You're a wonderful dancer," she told him.

"Thanks."

"I'll bet you're wonderful at everything you do."

"I . . . I try," he stammered, nearly choking on the words.

Once they were back at their table the laughs never stopped coming. Neither did the drinks. It went on for hours. Then they finally left. To go to another club.

That next one was different from the first. It was considerably more noisy, smoky, and crowded. They all had a great time there. Laughing. Drinking. Prometheus danced with Eris who again kept hanging on his every word, not to mention his body.

The club after that was different still. It was there that

Eris didn't dance with him. For one whole number. On that one she got up on the stage and danced with the band. Then at the end of the song she jumped off the stage into his waiting arms. That's when they first kissed. Prometheus thought it was wonderful. And kind of scary. The second and third and fourth and fifth kisses were just as wonderful. They were strangely not scary at all. But they were strange in another way. They made him forget all about having kissed Juanita. They also made him forget entirely the dreams he had often had of kissing Helen.

When they came out of the next club Durk actually seemed a little drunk for once. Maybe more than just a little. Prometheus wasn't too sure about it though, since his own vision was kind of blurred at the time.

"You know what?" Durk asked, burping loudly. "I'd really like to be alone with this lady here." He hugged Pandora, burped again, and then pointed at the other couple. "But I don't know what to do about you two."

"We'll be fine," said Prometheus.

"You can bet on it," Eris added, putting a hand on his chest.

For some reason her words made Durk laugh loudly. In turn, his laughter caused Prometheus to hold his head which suddenly started aching. "Speaking of betting . . . " Durk drawled.

"Oh," snapped Eris, "does Prometheus have a game tomorrow?"

Prometheus just couldn't seem to follow the strange logic connecting what the two of them had just said, but somehow that didn't seem important. What was important was how dizzy he was feeling. He leaned on Eris. She smiled and helped hold him up.

"Yeah," Durk answered her, "tomorrow afternoon."

Prometheus had forgotten all about that. He was so sleepy that he seemed to have forgotten everything. Eris checked her diamond-studded watch. "Then maybe we better get him back to camp."

"But Pandora and me were—"

"*I'll* take him," said Eris.

"How?"

She nodded at a long line of cabs parked across the street. Durk stepped out and motioned for the first one in line to come over for them.

"Who's the game with?" Eris asked.

Prometheus burped. "Some team from the local community college."

"Can you beat them?"

"Easily."

Durk grinned and punched him lightly on the shoulder. "You'll *destroy* them!"

"Right!"

"I wish I could stay over," said Pandora, "to be there to cheer you on."

The taxi pulled up. Eris led Prometheus to it. As they were getting in she turned her head back to Pandora and winked. "Thanks, hon . . . but that won't be necessary."

Both women laughed. Strangely. Knowingly.

*   *   *

Prometheus didn't really remember much of the ride back to camp. Except, of course, for the fact that he never got there.

He did remember how there was a lot of laughing and a fair share of kissing and like stuff, but the specific details were still kind of fuzzy in his mind. The taxi seemed to have moved real slowly down the misty moonlit road. It was strange.

Eris took her tongue out of his ear for a moment to ask the taxi driver if they were near the camp yet. He replied that he thought they were. Prometheus pointed out the window over the driver's shoulder.

"It's just around the bend in the road after that motel up ahead."

"*Motel?*" Eris asked with great interest. "Really?"

Then she asked Prometheus something, but he forgot what it was, except that he seemed to remember it was something rather agreeable. Then she told him something, but he forgot whatever that was too. Then she spoke to the driver. He remembered that. She told him to pull into the motel parking lot. The driver drove up beside the office and kind of snickered when Eris had to help Prometheus out of the cab.

"How much?" Prometheus asked the driver.

He checked his meter. "Thirty-one seventy-five."

"What?" asked Prometheus, suddenly feeling the cold night air blowing across his face.

"Thirty-one dollars and seventy-five cents . . . plus tip!"

Prometheus started fumbling hopelessly through his wallet. "Wow, I don't know what I was thinking of. I didn't think it would be that much. As a matter of fact I didn't even think—"

"It's okay," said Eris.

She reached into her purse and took out a crisp fifty dollar bill which she handed to the driver. Then she started leading Prometheus into the office, telling the driver to keep the change. He tipped his beret and grinned for the first time since they'd gotten into his taxi.

"Lady, if you ever need transportation again, make sure you come to me. I go anywhere, absolutely anywhere at all. My name's Al . . . Al Charon. I own this cab company."

He pointed up to the roof of the taxi. The brightly lighted red sign there read: "Styx Cab." Somehow that seemed strange to Prometheus. Somehow he thought it should have meant something to him, but just then he simply couldn't remember what it might be. For the life of him he couldn't remember.

CHAPTER TEN

P ROMETHEUS WOKE UP TO THE SOUND OF A BASKETBALL. IT WAS BEING BOUNCED against a tree somewhere in the woods outside the motel cabin. The sound was somewhat distant at first, but it was steadily getting closer. Prometheus looked around. Eris was sleeping soundly beside him. That was strange. He didn't remember getting into bed with her. Or anything else for that matter. He got up slowly and carefully so he wouldn't wake her, then went over to the window and looked out.

It was Hobie. He was coming up a forest path using a tattered old ball on the trees in the same way he had shown Prometheus in one of their drills at the music camp . . . bouncing it up at different heights and angles to sharpen your reflexes on the return. It was a good exercise. He was enjoying himself. Then he spotted Prometheus at the window and waved.

Prometheus went back to the bed, grabbed his clothes, and quickly started dressing. Just then Eris woke up.

"Where are you going?"

"To play basketball."

"Is it time for the game already?" she asked sleepily.

"No. This is just for fun."

"You don't have to go out for that," Eris said, slowly slipping the sheet off her naked body.

Prometheus thought he had never seen such an enchanting sight before, and he meant really *never* before . . . since he couldn't remember just how she'd ever gotten so naked in the first place. The greatest wonder of it all was probably the mystery. He'd always been a great mystery fan. He just stood there staring.

"What are you waiting for?" she asked.

The truth was that he didn't know. Oh sure, his head hurt like hell and he still couldn't really see completely straight. His stomach felt kind of funny too. And his teeth. And his hair. But he wasn't sure it was any of that. He kept hearing the sound of the basketball bouncing against the trees outside. It was strange. Like he couldn't make up his mind or something.

Then Eris smiled and licked her full red moist lips. Then he made up his mind and returned to bed.

*   *   *

They were late getting to the gym. Prometheus said they could have walked there, but Eris insisted on taking a cab. It turned out to be the same guy as the night before. Al Charon of Styx Taxi. Prometheus wondered if the man ever slept. He only charged them two dollars this time. Which was strange since he had to come all the way out from town. Prometheus guessed it was still worth his while though since Eris tipped him twenty-three. The camp parking lot was packed and cars were still coming in while long lines of people were disappearing into the gym.

The game was just about to start so Prometheus had to rush to the locker room. Eris gave him a final kiss. As he turned away from her he looked up into the bleachers. Helen was sitting there with Hobie. They were staring strangely at him. A few rows over he spotted his mother and Athena. They were staring too. Hell, he had completely forgotten that they were coming up.

It looked like a tough game from the start. The camp team really had to struggle against the older, taller, and generally much rougher looking community college players. Somehow the camp managed to hold their own, but at times just barely. Prometheus only scored eight points in the first half. He was badly fouled several times, but he missed all his foul shots. The opposition was good. He was terrible. Three cups of black coffee at the motel had helped a little, but he still didn't have a clear head.

He knew he looked bad, and he wondered what Hobie thought. Eris didn't seem to mind though. She was sitting with Durk and every time Prometheus looked up there he saw her laughing. Once he saw her holding Durk's arm and whispering in his ear. Then Durk was laughing too. She never seemed to be paying much attention to the game at all.

The buzzer sounded ending the first half. They were behind 47 to 43. All the players left the court. Durk joined the camp team in the locker room.

Prometheus was surprised that he didn't seem at all angry about the way they'd been playing. He just gave some advice on how they could improve in the second half.

It was almost time to resume play when Prometheus saw Gaia and Athena in line for a drink at the water fountain. He thought he'd surprise them so he went over and got in line several places behind them. They didn't spot him.

"Is something wrong, Mom?" he heard Athena ask.

"I don't know, honey. Your brother seems different somehow." "Maybe it's just the way they play basketball up here," Athena suggested.

Just then the buzzer sounded. Prometheus had to get back on the court before he could say hello to his family. Durk shot him a victory sign from the side-lines. Eris blew him a kiss.

The second half was different. Prometheus took Durk's advice and started using what he'd learned in practice. It all worked just as well in a real game. Prometheus was quickly emerging as the star of the game—coming on really strong, fighting when he had to, cheating when he felt it was called for, generally grandstanding his way to become the top scorer on either team. He got called for some fouls, but he got away with a lot more. Thanks to Durk.

Prometheus glanced up into the bleachers from time to time to see what effect his playing was having on the others. Their reactions varied greatly. To say the least. Hobie now looked mad as hell. Gaia was worried. Athena surprised. Helen concerned. Durk and Eris contented and happy. For no reason that he could imagine several fights had broken out in other parts of the stands and various fans were arguing loudly with each other. There were shouts and curses directed not only at each other but at the players and officials as well. He'd never experienced such behavior to this degree at high school games, especially not in a non-league game like this that meant nothing in terms of any ratings or championships. It was strange.

Pretty soon Prometheus' spirit of playing was catching. Several of his team-mates started imitating his style. One of them even injured an opposing player bad enough to have him carried out of the gym on a stretcher. There were plenty of other fouls and even a couple fights between players, but the camp team was now consistently outscoring the players on the community college squad.

One of them had been crowding Prometheus badly. He was only about an inch taller, but built like a bull and impossible for Prometheus to evade. Prometheus had wanted to get him for most of the second half. His chance finally came with only seconds to go. Prometheus had noticed how the players from both teams were jammed up so tight that they were often blocking the view of the officials. It was exactly what Prometheus needed. The player had just gotten the ball when Prometheus clipped him. Now *he* had the ball. The player had a bloody nose. More fights and arguments were breaking out in the stands.

The crowd was counting down the remaining time as Prometheus broke free of the jam-up and made his shot from near the center of the court. The ball sailed through the net just as the buzzer sounded ending the game. Prometheus' team won. Final score: 100 to 74. The gym went wild. The camp team was swamped by family and friends. The other team was complaining to the officials and showing them the bloodied nose of the player Prometheus had intentionally elbowed. The officials were all shaking their heads. What could they do? They hadn't actually seen anything so what choice did they have but to do nothing? What choice had Prometheus given them?

Eris ran out onto the court, threw her arms around Prometheus, and started seriously kissing him right there. Then she hung on his arm as Durk came up behind him and slapped him on the back.

"You did it!" he shouted. "Who *told* you that you could do it?"

"*You* did!" Prometheus shouted back as soon as he had a free lip.

"Damn right I did!"

"How does it feel?" asked Eris.

"It feels just . . . " he paused for an instant when he noticed Hobie and Helen approaching. "Uh . . . it feels just wonderful."

"No," said Hobie.

Durk turned to look at him. "What's the matter, old man?"

"There was *no* wonder in it. No wonder at all."

"We beat them," Prometheus said.

"So?"

"We beat them by twenty-six points."

"So?"

Durk and Eris each grabbed one of Prometheus' arms and led him off through the still growing crowd of well-wishers. As they did so it was Durk who answered Hobie's question. "*So* you're just going to be the best damn player this camp ever turned out."

"The *damned* best!" emphasized Eris.

The crush of bodies was slowing them down. Prometheus saw Gaia and Athena trying to make their way to him, but they were all being pushed and pulled in opposite directions by the swelling currents of people all around them. The undertow was dragging Hobie and Helen right after Prometheus, although he sensed that wasn't their own intention. They were only a few feet away at one point and Prometheus could hear them talking to each other.

"No wonder at all in such a performance," Hobie intoned solemnly.

"And no music," added Helen.

*　　*　　*

The Chinese restaurant in town looked packed and Prometheus was afraid they wouldn't get in. At the very least the long line waiting outside would probably mean an hour's wait. But his fears proved groundless. They got right in and were immediately seated despite the large size of their party— Prometheus and Eris,

Durk, most of the team and their girl friends.

They had just ordered when Prometheus spotted Gaia and Athena sitting in a small corner booth. When he rose to go back to them he noticed that Eris got up with him, but then Durk caught her arm and whispered something to her. She sat down again. Frowning.

"Hi, mom . . . " said Prometheus, " . . . sis."

His mother looked up from the menu. "We weren't sure this was the restaurant you meant."

"This is it. The only Chinese place in town. How do you like it?"

"It's big," she said.

"Yeah. Say, how did you like the way I—"

"I wish our place was even half this size."

"Right, Mom, but what did you think of how I—"

"We'd be rich if we could only get half the customers they have here tonight."

"*What did you think of the game?*"

"It was kind of violent."

Athena smiled. "You sure scored a lot, bro!"

"I'm glad one of you noticed."

"What I notice," said Gaia, "is that you're still standing beside our booth. Aren't you going to sit down?"

She indicated a spot next to Athena. Prometheus stole a quick glance back at Eris. She smiled and waved. "Uh, yeah . . . sure thing, Mom," Prometheus said as he sat down.

"Who's that girl?" asked Athena.

"Her name's Eris . . . Eris Yin."

"She your girl-friend?"

"Well, uh . . . yeah, I guess you could say that."

"She's very beau . . . ti . . . ful," Athena said with a mocking tone just before she started giggling.

"That she is," Prometheus agreed.

"And a few years older than you, I would imagine," said his mother.

"I don't know, Mom."

"Maybe more than just a few," she added.

Prometheus felt he just had to change the subject. He asked Athena what she thought of his last basket. She lifted up both her hands and they high-fived, slapping their hands together with a resounding whack. Then they both burst out laughing. All that had little effect on their mother though. She was still keeping an eye on Eris.

"Where did you meet her, Prometheus?"

"Up here."

"*How* did you meet her?"

"Through a friend," he replied.

"And just which friend would that be?"

"Durk."

"Oh, that one's a friend now?"

"People change, Mom."

She stared at him, through him. "So I've noticed."

What *Prometheus* noticed just then was some kind of commotion over at the door. Hobie had entered and was gently pushing his way through the crowd still waiting in line. Now his way was being blocked by a hostess at least a head taller than him.

"Do you have a reservation?" she asked him.

"No."

"In that case, sir, I'm afraid you'll just have to wait in line like everyone else."

"I don't want to *eat* here," he shouted back at her.

"Then exactly what *do* you want?"

"*Him!*" Hobie shouted, pointing at Prometheus.

He tried coming over to their booth, but again the tall hostess stood in his way. Of course she had no chance, thought Prometheus. No more chance than he ever had. Than any mere human being would have. First, Hobie smiled at her. When she smiled back, he feinted left. Then he feinted right.

She moved that way. Bad mistake. He feinted left again. She fell for that one too, putting herself completely off balance and leaning the wrong way as he finally stopped feinting and quickly walked around her. On her right side.

Prometheus saw Durk get up and follow behind him. At a safe distance. Hobie didn't appear to see him, but Prometheus suspected that appearances could be deceiving. They usually were with Hobie. Prometheus stood up when the old man reached the booth and ignored the hand offered him to shake.

"Hi, Hobie. I—"

"You got somethin' I want, boy."

"As always," Durk said quietly.

Hobie ignored him. "Somethin' that's mine."

"What?" asked Prometheus.

"You know damn well!"

Prometheus shook his head. "No I don't. What—" but then, looking deeply into the old man's eye, he *did* know. "The ball?"

"Damn right the ball!" Hobie shouted.

"You want it back?"

"Of course I want it back!"

"Why?"

"Cause it's bein' wasted."

"On me?" asked Prometheus.

Hobie nodded. "At least you got that much straight. Now, where the hell is it?"

"Not on him, obviously," said Durk. Again Hobie ignored him.

"Back at camp."

"Okay, then. I'll be expecting it in the morning. *First thing* in the morning."

With that Hobie turned and walked right out, brushing past Durk who tried getting in his way, and feinting his way around the tall hostess who didn't.

"Why do you take that kind of stuff from him?" asked Durk.

"Well," said Prometheus, "it *is* his ball."

"So?"

Just then Athena seemed to remember the computer print-out sheets with which she'd been fidgeting. Prometheus had noticed she had them with her at the game and had been waving them at him.

"You'll like this, Prometheus," she said. "I think I finally figured a way to—"

"And I lied to him," Prometheus told Durk.

"About what?"

"The ball. It's not back at camp."

"Where is it then?"

Athena tried again to get into the conversation. "It was really a tough one, but I checked all my calculations and—"

"In the trunk of your car," Prometheus told Durk.

"Of course," said Athena, "at first I didn't even think there was any way to compute all those simultaneous—"

Durk snapped his fingers. "That's right. I forgot."

"Let's go get it," Prometheus said, stepping out from behind the booth.

"What's the rush? The old man did say first thing in the morning, didn't he?

"Yeah, but I don't want to even take a chance on forgetting it again."

Athena angrily threw her papers down on the table. Prometheus quickly kissed her and his mother good-night, then left with Durk right behind him. Eris got up and followed them as they passed her table.

*   *   *

Durk opened the trunk and Prometheus took out the blue ball. It glowed brightly in the night air.

"How pretty!" exclaimed Eris. "Can I have it?"

"It's not mine," Prometheus told her.

"So?"

"So I'm going to return it to its owner."

"In the morning," said Durk. "You could at least let her *look* at it now, couldn't you?"

Not waiting for a reply, Eris took the ball from Prometheus and held it up to her face so that she was bathed in its blue light. She smiled. "What makes it glow?"

Prometheus confessed that he had no idea.

Durk laughed. "*I* know," he said sarcastically. "It must be . . . *magic*."

"Oh yes!" Eris squealed with delight.

Durk put his arm around the shoulder of Prometheus. "Tell you what, old buddy, give the ball back tonight. It'll make you feel better. Take my car."

"Oh no," Prometheus protested. "I couldn't—"

"It's the least I can do. C'mon, I'll show you how to drive this thing. It's got a couple special features you might not be familiar with."

Prometheus followed him around to the driver's side. Eris was playfully tossing the ball up in the air and then catching it with one hand. Prometheus got behind the wheel and Durk started instructing him in some of the intricacies of his customized Mercedes. Just then Prometheus happened to glance into the rear-view mirror and saw something strange. Something really strange. Something that simply couldn't be. In fact, when he blinked and looked again it wasn't happening. He figured that somehow he must have imagined it.

For what he had seen was the blue ball spinning wildly on its own in mid-air several inches above the outstretched hand of Eris Yin.

CHAPTER ELEVEN

THE CAR DROVE LIKE A DREAM. PROMETHEUS THOUGHT THAT HE ACTUALLY handled it much more carefully than Durk had seemed to. Eris sat up front next to the driver's seat, smoking a cigarette in a long ivory holder and constantly switching stations on the radio until she found some Gangsta Rap that she liked.

She had had immediate objections to both of the CDs Prometheus had tried to play earlier. They were ones he had gotten from Hobie. On the first, Louis Armstrong had barely finished playing his opening nine measure improvised cadenza to "West End Blues" when Eris burst out laughing and insisted that he turn off such outdated junk. The second was "Saeta" from Miles Davis' *Sketches of Spain* album. She insisted he turn that one off because it was too dreary, although he remembered how much he had enjoyed listening to it with Helen at her pool and how she claimed it was one of the most moving and inspiring trumpet solos she had ever heard.

"Could you lower that just a bit?" asked Prometheus.

Eris turned off the radio. "That better?"

"Much."

"Thanks for taking me along."

"No problem."

"You're sure it's not out of your way?"

He shook his head. "No. Your motel's first, then my camp, then Hobie's."

"He seems like a strange old man."

"That's how he seems all right," Prometheus said with a smile.

"How old is he?"

"Old!"

"How many years?"

"Damned if I know. He's said things that make me think he's over ninety, over a hundred even."

"I think he's even older than that," said Eris, " . . . much, much older."

Prometheus had no trouble making it up to Eris' motel. He stopped in the parking lot and let her out. As soon as he had seen her enter her cabin he started backing up in order to turn around. Suddenly he heard her screaming. He stopped the car again and raced for her door.

Rushing inside he found her standing calmly in the dark in the center of the room. Naked.

"What is it?" he asked.

"Just this," she replied, throwing her arms around him and almost literally smothering him with kisses. After several moments he broke free and headed for the door. As he exited Eris stood frozen in place, smiling wryly and slowly shaking her head.

"Sometimes you just never know," she said to herself.

A moment later he returned with the blue ball. He held it up for her to see, then rolled it over into a corner, and went to her.

"Sometimes you do," she thought as he pulled her body tightly against his.

*   *   *

The outdoor basketball courts were already frying in the early morning sun. Prometheus was practicing hard with the other players from the camp's winning team. Durk and Eris watched from the sidelines. They were the first ones to see Hobie approaching rapidly from the road. Then Prometheus spotted him and looked startled.

"It's still morning," said Hobie, "but *first thing* has long since passed."

"I'm sorry," Prometheus mumbled, slapping his forehead as he suddenly remembered what he had forgotten.

"Again?"

"Uh, yeah, maybe I could just . . . " Prometheus began, looking over at Durk.

Durk nodded. "Sure, go get the geezer's ball."

"Thanks. I'll be right back."

*   *   *

Hobie and Prometheus walked together along the dusty road from the camp to the motel. Silently at first. Then Hobie spoke.

"You have to ask his permission to leave?"

"Yeah, it was during practice and he's my teacher."

"Once I was your teacher."

"You still are. I just—"

"No. No longer. You have chosen a different path . . . a much different path."

*   *   *

They reached the motel and entered the cabin where Prometheus started looking for the ball. It wasn't in the room where he'd rolled it. He looked under the rumpled bed. Hobie just looked around generally suspicious.

"Is this part of your camp?" Hobie asked.

"No, not exactly."

"How do you stay here then?"

"I have special permission."

"From who . . . your *teacher*?" asked Hobie.

"No. Well, not exactly, but Durk has connections and—"

Prometheus was searching the room more fanatically now. Hobie found a woman's sheer black stocking on the bed and held it up to the light. It matched the black silk dress and the wisp of black silk thong panties Eris had worn to the restaurant and left lying on the floor. "I see . . . "

"Where the hell is that damn ball?" Prometheus asked desperately.

Hobie was smoothing out the stocking. "I don't think you're going to find it here."

"Sure I will," said Prometheus. "Last night I—"

"She can be quite lovely, boy."

"You mean Eris?"

Hobie burst into laughter. "Is that what she's calling herself again?"

"That's her name."

"It surely is," Hobie said, still chuckling.

"What's so funny?"

"You really don't know?"

"No. Tell me."

"Ask your mother."

"Why?"

"Because she's a woman . . . a Greek woman."

*　　*　　*

Prometheus returned to practice alone. Hobie had left him at the cabin.

"The old man get what he wanted?" asked Durk.

"No."

"How come?"

"I couldn't find the ball."

Durk shook his head. "Too bad. Say, you had some visitors while you were gone."

"Who?"

"They're over at the cafeteria with Eris."

*　　*　　*

Durk went with him. When they entered the cafeteria they found Gaia and Athena sitting with Eris at a table and laughing. Prometheus went over to his mother and kissed her on the cheek. She took his hand and clasped it between her own.

"What happened to you last night? We thought you forgot all about us."

"I'm sorry, Mom. I—"

"It's all my fault," said Eris. "I'm afraid I was the one who kept him out to the wee small hours."

"You thought I forgot you?"

"Yeah," Athena seconded her mother's opinion, "and I never got to show you how I—

She shuffled the computer print-out sheets before her on the table. Eris picked them up and waved them right under Prometheus' nose. "Do you know that your little sister here is a real genius?"

"I know," said Prometheus.

Athena beamed as Eris hugged her. "Well, what can I say?"

"I'd say that I'm kind of hungry," said Durk. "Anybody else want something to eat? My treat."

Gaia shook her head as she indicated the empty dishes in front of her and her daughter. "Oh, no thanks. We've both had plenty already."

"I could use another coke," said Athena.

Durk turned towards Prometheus. "And for the All-Star?"

"Burger and fries, my good man."

Gaia then reconsidered. "Uh, maybe a refill of my coffee . . . If it's not too much trouble."

"No trouble at all."

"Let me help you get it," said Eris.

The two of them headed over to the food line all the way across the huge room. Prometheus sat down at the table with his mother and sister.

"Well, mom, how do you like it up here?"

"It's nice," she replied, " . . . very nice."

"Is that all you can say?

"What else?"

"That it's great . . . fantastic . . . wonderful!"

"Is it?"

"Absolutely."

"Are you happy?"

"Sure."

"Why, Prometheus?" asked Gaia, "just why are you happy here?"

Prometheus smiled. "Just look at me, mom. I've gotten bigger and stronger in just a matter of weeks thanks to their weight training, and of course I'm playing the best basketball of my life."

"Hobie doesn't think so."

"What's he know?"

"Plenty," Athena chimed in.

"Oh yeah? Maybe he does, but what good was it doing me? Sure, he *knows* plenty, but his whole style . . . his whole way of approaching the game is really kind of . . . well, strange!"

His mother stared silently for just a moment."Have you seen Helen lately?"

"No. Not real lately."

"Too bad. She's such a nice girl, a nice *young* girl."

"Listen, mom," began Prometheus, his voice rising, "I really don't like you implying anything about Eris or her—."

Durk and Eris returned with the food and distributed it to everyone. "Here you go," said Durk. "I think we'll get another table so that you folks can have a little privacy."

"Oh no, please . . . " Prometheus objected.

"It's probably best," said Eris

They moved over to another table nearby and turned their backs on Prometheus and his family, but they were still close enough so that they could hear every word spoken.

"For some strange I kind of like her," said Athena, "though I can't really say why. It's sort of confusing."

"Who?"

"Eris."

"So do I," Prometheus agreed.

"But I like Helen a whole lot better. So does Mom. Don't you, Mom?"

Gaia nodded. "Have you heard anything yet about one of those scholar-ships?"

"Not officially," said Prometheus, "but Durk says it's a sure thing if I keep playing the way I have been."

"Oh god, I hope you get it," Gaia whispered, looking ready to cry.

Prometheus touched her arm. "What's wrong, mom?"

"It's the restaurant."

"What about it?"

"We might lose it."

"Why?"

"Bills are up," she said shrugging, "business is down."

"I'll come home with you today, Mom. I'll get a job. College can wait. I'm not—"

"No. It won't wait. If there's even the slightest chance that you can go to college now, then you go."

"But mom-"

"It's what your father would have wanted."

*   *   *

Prometheus stood with his mother and sister in the small crowd of people waiting for the camp shuttle. Eris and Durk pulled up in his car.

"Where you folks headed?" asked Durk.

"Back to the hotel in town to get their things," Prometheus explained, "and then they've got to catch the last bus down to Philadelphia."

Durk shook his head. "I'll take them."

"Thanks," said Prometheus. "The bus leaves in less than an hour."

"Forget the bus. I'll take them all the way."

"Oh no," said Gaia. "It's much too far to have you drive all the way to the city."

"Not at all. I'm going home tonight. It's just a few blocks from your restaurant."

"He can use the company," Eris said, climbing out of the front of the car and then helping Gaia and Athena get in the back.

"Where were you going?" Prometheus asked her.

"The motel," she said, "but I can just as easily walk there from here."

"Durk, this is really wonderful of you to take my mom and Athena."

"It's nothing."

"Thank you," said Gaia.

"Can we play the radio?" Athena asked.

He answered by turning it on full blast to a Country and Western sta-tion. Athena squealed with delight as the car raced out of camp. Prometheus started walking with Eris back to the motel. He could hear his sister's laugh-ter quickly fading away as the Mercedes disappeared from view.

"That was really nice of Durk, wasn't it?"

"Yes," Prometheus agreed, "but you're sure you don't mind walking?"

"No."

"You're pretty nice yourself, Eris."

She laughed. "I'm glad you noticed."

"It's not that short a walk, you know?"

"That's okay. I don't mind the exercise, not that I *really need* any extra workouts all that much . . . " she said touching his shoulder. "Not with you around."

*   *   *

The instant they had entered her cabin they grabbed each other and clung together kissing passionately. It went on so long that Prometheus finally had to break away in order to catch his breath.

"Wow!"

Again Eris laughed. "And you dared refer to me as simply . . . 'pretty nice'."

"My mistake," he conceded.

They went at it again.

*   *   *

With the music continuing to blare and Athena laughing louder than ever, Durk's car quickly passed through the town and headed out towards the highway below.

*   *   *

"There was somethin' I wanted to ask you," said Prometheus, his speech slightly slurred. He was curled up with Eris on the bed watching a loud music video on TV as they ate pizza and drank beer. He was dressed only in his shorts. She in her red satin string-bikini panties and matching bra.

"What?"

"I don't remember,"

"Well," said Eris, "the answer is definitely . . . *yes!*"

Prometheus didn't get it. Not at first. "Wha do ya mean . . . the answer is—" Then the realization dawned on him and he burst out laughing. She joined him, then handed him another beer. He looked at it dumbly, then held up the can in his other hand.

"But I already have a beer," he said with a burp.

"So?"

Again he laughed uproariously, spitting beer out of his mouth, then choking. She patted his back. Hard. He laughed once more as he started drinking alternately from one can to the other.

"Hey, it's getting dark," he said, glancing out the window.

"So?"

"How're you getting home?"

"I am home, Prometheus."

"No, no, I mean . . . " he tried explaining, again slurring his words and shaking his head to clear it, "how're you going to get back to the city to-night?"

"I'm not."

"But you . . . "

"I like it up here so I've decided to stay on for a while. Do you have any objections to that, Prometheus?"

"Hell no!" he shouted happily. Then he burped again.

*　　*　　*

Durk edged his car slowly up to the curb beside the restaurant and parked. He got out and quickly went around to open the back door for Gaia. She tried carrying the sleeping Athena, but the child was too heavy for her. Durk, however, had no trouble picking up Athena. He carried her with ease as he followed Gaia up to their apartment.

*　　*　　*

Prometheus and Eris were sleeping peacefully together in each other's arms when he suddenly stirred and got out of bed. He wandered naked around the room searching it for something, and mumbling to himself as he moved in the dark, his voice a slurred mixture of being more than half-asleep and still almost half-drunk.

" . . . must be here . . . somewhere . . . it's gotta . . . "

Eris stirred and opened one eye. "What are you doing?"

"I remember now," he said.

"Remember what?"

"What I wanted to ask you."

"And what's that, my darling?"

He coughed. "Where's the ball?"

"Which ball is that?" she asked, sitting up attentively and letting the sheets fall from her perfectly formed and now quite naked breasts.

"Aw, you know . . . Hobie's . . . blue . . . glows in dark."

"You're dreaming, Prometheus. A *blue* ball?"

"Yeah . . . blue basketball . . . Hobie's . . . around here somewhere."

She laughed. "And it *glows in the dark*?"

"Yeah . . . glows."

"You're dreaming, my darling," she said, "*and* you're still drunk. "Come on back to bed."

"No, no . . . gotta find it . . . return to Hobie."

"There's no such ball," she said flatly.

Prometheus stopped his search and looked down at her sumptuous nude body in the bed. "But you . . . you saw it . . . didn't you?"

"No."

"Sure you did. You even held it."

"Did I?"

He looked confused. "I thought you did . . . back in town . . . that night when I took it out of Durk's trunk."

"Durk has a trunk?" asked Eris. "What is he . . . an elephant or something?"

"No, no," Prometheus answered, laughing loudly at the thought, then holding his head in agony, "I mean the trunk of his car."

"Durk has a car?"

He stared at her wide-eyed. "Of course he has a car! Why do you even ask? You've ridden in it."

"Have I?"

"You *know* you have!

"Do I?"

"Where's Hobie's ball?" Prometheus asked, stumbling across the floor as he resumed his search.

"There is no ball, Prometheus. There is no Durk and there is no Hobie. Durk and Hobie are both *you*, Prometheus."

"You're crazy, Eris."

"There is no Eris, Prometheus."

"You're just plain nuts!"

"Am I?"

"Gotta find it."

"You can't find it, Prometheus. The ball is imaginary."

"No, no . . . it's real . . . it must be real."

"*Real?*" she asked, her voice deepening, "real like *this?*"

He turned back towards the bed and saw Eris playing with the blue ball. It was glowing brighter than ever as it spun in the air just inches above her face. She laughed as she grabbed the ball with both hands and kissed it. Then she placed the ball on the pillow beside her. Prometheus rubbed his eyes in disbelief. "What the hell?!"

"Come back to bed, Prometheus."

"Where'd you find it?"

"Find what?"

"That," he replied, pointing at the ball.

"This?" she asked, taking the pillow from beneath the ball and holding it over her head. "Why, it was here all along."

"No, not that . . . the *ball*."

"There is no ball, Prometheus."

He walked over to the bed and carefully reached down to take the ball between his hands. "Then what do you call this?"

Before his eyes the blue ball seemed to start shrinking in size as both its color and glow faded away. It transformed into the face of Eris Yin who was kissing his hands.

"Me," she said.

The shock both woke and sobered him. "I don't understand."

"I know, darling."

"The ball was just—"

"But more and more there's something you are starting to understand very well."

"What's that?"

"This," she whispered, kissing him fully on the mouth.

He resisted her at first, but then he grasped her wildly and began raining kisses all over her breasts and thighs and belly. Her laughter echoed in his ears as she urged him on with both her hands and her legs.

*　　*　　*

Hobie was staring out the window of the music camp's kitchen. He had been watching the camp's Chinese cook for several minutes. That short stocky man stood at the edge of the woods some twenty yards away. He was dressed in the white pants and shirt of his chef's uniform and he was moving his arms and legs in very graceful slow motion patterns that inscribed circles in the air around him. It was as if he were swimming in the thick morning mist coming in off the lake.

Suddenly the man smiled and motioned for Hobie to join him. That was strange. The chef shouldn't have been able to see him. Not at that distance. Not through the tiny darkened window that still lay in the shadows.

Still, Hobie had been summoned. So he had to go. The man never interrupted his movements as Hobie came out of the kitchen and walked towards him.

"Good morning."

"Good morning to you sir," the cook replied in a rather low gruff voice, his native Mandarin accented in a clipped British manner.

"What's that you're doing?" asked Hobie. "It kind of looks something like T'ai Chi Ch'uan."

That made the other man grin as he nodded while continuing his long series of movements. "Yes, yes. T'ai Chi. You recognize this form?"

"Well, not exactly. Some of the movements remind me of the old Yang style, but others have that distinctively high stance of the Sun school."

"Excellent!" exclaimed the cook. "You must know T'ai Chi very well."

"No, sir. Not hardly at all. I've just seen it done here and there from time to time . . . like I have a lot of things in my life."

"Well, you welcome to join me. Please just follow along. Don't worry about making each movement and posture precisely right. Just get feel of thing and let it flow through you."

Hobie smiled as he proceed to do as suggested. He'd been right again. As always. The way people moved was usually the best clue of all. Of course he had noticed the cook before. Back on his very first day in camp, even before he had started work. Actually he had noticed the man's cooking before he ever saw him in the flesh. The cooking was good. Exceptionally good. Amazingly good. So good that Hobie had a hard time remembering just where or when he had ever tasted anything quite so good before. It later turned out that it didn't matter what style or nationality of cooking the man did. It was all the same. Good. Wonderfully good. Strangely good. Whether his native Chinese cuisine in either Mandarin, Cantonese, or Sze Chuan—or Italian or French or American or Mexican or Greek—it was all excellent.

Then Hobie had met him at that morning's staff meeting and learned that his name was Chang Sam Fong. Hobie had immediately liked his face. Large and round with little twinkling eyes and a sly smile despite an otherwise somewhat sad and world-weary appearance. His skin seemed tough and weather beaten and he had a sparse scraggly beard. He stood only a bit taller than Hobie, but was heavier and looked immensely stronger. His age could have been anywhere between fifty and seventy.

"You are the one called Hobie?" Chang now asked, lifting his right leg with infinite slowness, then turning it widely to the side to kick out with the sole of his foot.

"Yeah, that's me."

"Hobie-the-wonder, if I remember correctly."

Hobie chuckled. "Not quite. Just plain old Hobie Wonder . . . whether I really am one or not is something folks got to decide for themselves."

"Is good name. What nationality . . . American?"

"Uh, yeah . . . for now."

Even though Chang was concentrating on his own movements he couldn't help but notice how adept Hobie was at following him. That was unusual. Strange, even. T'ai Chi was the most complex and deceptive style of all the martial arts. It normally took years just to learn the basic form with any degree of proficiency. Yet here was a little old black man not only matching many of the most subtle postures, but also showing a great affinity for the much more important and difficult aspects like relaxation and breathing.

Hobie was having fun. Even though he was concentrating on trying to follow Chang's intricate movements, he was also remembering how he had spotted the essence of that very grace when he had first seen the chef carrying huge heaping trays of food from the kitchen out through the crowded dining hall. It was all the same. And it was beautiful. As it always was.

*   *   *

Runners and bicyclists passed by each other in opposite directions as they raced through the morning sun beating down on the motel parking lot. Inside the cabin Eris was busy cooking breakfast in the kitchenette. Prometheus snored away in deep sleep as he lay sprawled out on the bed. Eventually the sizzle and smell of the bacon and eggs reached through to him. Suddenly he awoke with a start, sober now but with a tremendous hang-over.

"Eris?"

"Right over here."

"How did you—"

He looked all around the cabin, only gradually starting to become reoriented to the surroundings. Eris was there smiling sweetly at him from behind the stove.

"Breakfast will be ready soon, darling."

"Where's the ball?" asked Prometheus, looking first under the sheets, then under the bed.

"Which ball, Prometheus . . . oh, you mean that pretty blue glowing one you took out of Durk's trunk and brought out here that night?"

"Yes, yes!"

"It was a strange ball . . . very strange and wonderful."

"You remember it then?" he asked.

"Of course I remember. Do you want coffee or tea? I'm afraid the coffee will have to be instant."

"What I want is the ball! Where is it?"

She shrugged. "I have no idea."

"Last night when I woke up," Prometheus started asking, "when we talked and you—"

"But Prometheus, you slept straight through last night. Soundly. So did I."

CHAPTER TWELVE

"WHAT'S THE SECRET OF YOUR COOKIN?" HOBIE ASKED AS CHANG SERVED him yet another portion of French Toast.

The two of them were sitting alone in the now deserted kitchen. All the campers had finished their breakfast and their dishes were now being automatically scrubbed in the commercial size washers.

"Secret?"

"Yeah, what's the magical secret behind the great taste of all your food?"

"I don't know."

"Aw, c'mon now, Chang, you can tell me."

"But there are no secrets. Just relax and do things the right way."

"So *that's* the secret then," offered Hobie.

Chang looked surprised. "Maybe it is. Yes, do a good job. Do your best. That is whole secret."

Hobie was pleased. More pleased than Chang could possibly imagine from the simple nod and smile the older man gave him. He liked having Hobie around. It wasn't just that he was such a good worker, although he certainly was that and more. It was because he was such a good conversationalist. But no, that wasn't exactly right. Hobie was a great listener. He did tell Chang a few things about that strange boy Prometheus and what great hopes he had for him, but Hobie actually revealed very little about himself. What he did do was to somehow get Chang to open up about his own life.

For some reason the chef actually told him nearly everything. That was something he hadn't been able to do with anyone else in well over a decade. Not since he had left China.

*   *   *

Things had gone badly for Chang after the Tiananmen Square massacre. He'd been lucky enough to survive it, but from that day forward he was always on the run. Many others he'd known there were fleeing too, but none of them had a nine year old daughter with them as he had. Not that little Chai Li ever complained. Even when they had to go days without food and often had to live out in open fields, hiding during the day and only daring to move on at night. She was as sweet as ever throughout it all. As sweet as her mother Jen-i had been.

Her mother who had been shot to death in the very first wave of the Army's initial onslaught, machine-gunned down while trying to protect one of the student demonstrators she had been tending.

She was Chief of Nursing at a Beijing hospital before she became a nurse to the students. As Chang himself had been the Master Chef at one of the city's finest restaurants before he volunteered as their cook. He'd seen her fall from nearly a block away and had just managed to reach her shattered lifeless body when the tanks came.

Fortunately Chai Li was staying with friends several blocks from the Square, but by the time he had gotten there everyone was already clearing out. He had snatched up a few of her things along with some of his own and they were soon running away from the noise and blood behind them.

They'd been moving and hiding for several weeks after that before eventually making their way far to the south where his wife had relatives. Chai Li had cried very little when he first told her of her mother's death, but each day from then on he'd hear her whimpering in her sleep as they lay hidden under bridges or in boxes at the ends of deserted alleys.

The relatives in the south were Jen-i's cousin and his family. They readily took him and Chai-li into their large household, despite the fact that the cousin's wife was a low level party functionary. Chang was tremendously grateful to them, but over the next month he noticed a growing change in their attitude. They were worried. By the second month they were outright scared. Chang's name wasn't at all high on the list of fugitives the government was scouring the country to find, but it was on it. Fortunately his daughter's wasn't.

The cousin convinced him that it would be best to leave China as soon as possible. That wouldn't be easy, but it could be arranged. Others had already escaped in the holds of freighters. There was another one scheduled to depart from Shanghai. They could get Chang up there and onto the ship within a few days. The problem was that the cramped quarters in the darkened hold were no place for a little girl. He didn't want to be separated from Chai Li, but it seemed like the best solution at the time. The cousin and his wife insisted that hiding his daughter would be much easier than continuing to hide him. Much easier and very much safer.

In the end he reluctantly agreed. A loosely organized local network of dissidents and their supporters would help get him to San Francisco. The cousin's wife swore that after the heat died down she had connections who could have Chai Li travel to Hong Kong. From there it would be an easy flight to America. She'd probably be rejoining her father in a matter of months, certainly within the a year. Besides, that would give him time to get himself established in the new country. It sounded okay to him at the time, but it didn't work out the way he had been promised. Not at all.

Chang hadn't seen his daughter now in over twelve years.

A game was already in progress when Prometheus arrived at the outdoor court. He asked for Durk, but was told that he hadn't gotten back yet from the city. As soon as Prometheus started playing, the game noticeably escalated in both speed and violence. His style was a totally vicious one now, even towards the players on his own side, despite the fact that it was just a practice game.

Durk's car pulled up on the road beside the court. He got out and went around to stand behind the back door on the passenger side where he motioned for Prometheus. Durk opened the door when Prometheus arrived. Out stepped a dapper dude in a dark business suit. He was tall and muscular, looked about sixty or so with his silvery hair, and had 'mob' written all over him.

"Prometheus," said Durk, "I'd like you to meet Jimmy Zeus. Jimmy, this is Prometheus Go."

"Glad to meet you, kid. I've heard a lot of great things about you," said Jimmy, his South Philadelphia accent so thick that even Prometheus had trouble understanding him.

Durk nodded. "Jimmy's always on the lookout for fresh athletic talent."

"Oh, you're with one of the colleges?" Prometheus asked.

"Not exactly," answered Zeus, laughing at the thought.

"But," Durk quickly added, "he's really helped some of our players over the years."

"How?"

Jimmy grinned, the tiny diamonds in his front teeth sparkling in the sun. "We'll talk later, kid. Right now I'm in the mood to watch some basketball."

Durk motioned for Prometheus to return to the game. He quickly did so. Jimmy stood watching the game as carefully as a hawk following its prey. He nodded and smiled slightly every time

Prometheus stole the ball or scored a basket, but he actually laughed aloud whenever he got away with a sneak foul or other illegal move.

"What did I tell you?" asked Durk.

"I'm impressed. He's good . . . *damn* good!"

"And this is just practice, Mr. Zeus. You ought to see him go to work in a real game. He's awesome."

"That's what Nick Ares told me."

"Yeah," said Durk, "and you gotta remember that Nick was only up here for Prometheus' *first* game. He's improved a lot since then. Now he even—"

Zeus put up his hand. "I told you I'm already impressed."

"I knew you would be, Mr. Zeus. You can always depend on me to scout out good prospects."

"Yeah, yeah, all that I know. The question is . . . will I be able to depend on this kid?"

"No problem."

"Listen Durk, you haven't uh . . . 'discussed' anything with him yet, have you?"

"No, sir."

"Then how the hell do you know this guy will even want to deal with me at all?"

Durk chuckled. "I've got *two* reasons to think so. Two very good, very precious reasons."

*　　*　　*

Prometheus entered the motel cabin with Durk. Zeus followed them, looking all around suspiciously. "Is this place secure?"

"Absolutely," said Durk.

Zeus spun around quickly as he caught the sound of the shower running in the bathroom. He angrily pointed towards it. "Somebody's in there!"

"It's nothing to worry about, boss."

"Hey, *you* don't tell *me* what's to worry about and what's not to worry about."

"Sorry."

"The reason I'm still around after such a long time, the reason I'm still out here operatin' my business today is precisely because I do know when to worry."

"Okay . . . " Durk whispered, subtly indicating Prometheus.

Zeus caught his cue. "Uh . . . what I mean to say is that this here's gotta be a matter of 'confidential' negotiations."

"And you're afraid of spies?" asked Prometheus.

"That's one word for them, kid."

The sounds of the shower stopped and the bathroom door opened. Eris came out in a short red bathrobe, drying her hair with a long towel. "Hi, everybody."

"Eris!" shouted Zeus, very pleasantly surprised.

She nodded and smiled. "Mr. Zeus."

"How you been, babe?"

"Wonderful . . . absolutely wonderful, thanks," she answered, "and yourself?"

"Oh, not bad . . . not bad at all. What the hell are *you* doin' all the way up here?"

She walked up close to him and whispered in his ear. "I'm on a mission."

"Oh yeah?" he asked, laughing with her. "So am I."

"I'm on a mission from the gods," Eris emphasized.

"Which ones, baby?"

They both laughed again. Much more loudly this time. As if they shared some great, profoundly humorous secret. Then he gave her a little hug and a kiss. Prometheus looked on with a mixture of jealousy and embarrassment. "Uh . . . would anyone like something to drink?" he asked.

"Sure, kid. You got any Scotch around here?"

"I don't think so."

"Go get some then. Eris and me got some catchin' up to do."

"I've got some dressing to do," she said.

"Not on my account, sweet-cheeks."

She pulled away from him, but he grabbed the bottom of her robe and tugged playfully at it. "Naughty, naughty, Mr. Zeus."

"That's me," Zeus said, " . . . all over."

Prometheus started moving towards Zeus, but Durk was quick in holding him back. "Let's go see if the bar's open yet."

*   *   *

Durk placed some bills on the counter as the bartender handed him a tray with a bottle and glasses on it. Prometheus was pacing before the bar and steaming.

"You settled down yet?" asked Durk.

"Just who the hell does he think he is?"

Durk put the tray back on the bar. "I guess not."

"Where does he know her from?

"Search me."

"When we go back I ought to—"

"When we go back what you ought to do is listen to what he can do for you," said Durk.

"I'm not interested in what—"

"And for your family."

"What about them?"

Durk picked up the tray again and led the way out of the bar. "Listen, I know it's none of my business, but it was a long drive back to the city and I got to talking with your mom about the restaurant. It's in big trouble, isn't it?"

"You're right."

"Well then, you really should—"

"You're right . . . it's none of your business."

Durk winced at the old joke. "Very funny, but not very helpful to your mom and sister."

"Hey, I can take care of them."

"Maybe you can . . . with Zeus's help."

"No way!"

"No way I can think of . . . " Durk said, shaking his head, "without him."

*   *   *

Prometheus sat silently with Durk and Zeus at the table. Eris was dressed now and sprawled out reading a newspaper on the bed. Zeus poured himself another generous portion of Scotch.

"So that's all there is to it, kid. Pretty simple, huh?"

"Yeah."

"What do you think of the plan?"

"Not much," said Prometheus.

"Why the hell not?"

"For one thing, I could get caught."

Zeus laughed. "For doin' what? Playin' basketball?"

"No," Prometheus said, "for shaving points."

"That's the beauty of it, kid. You don't have to do all that much shavin'. What're those figures again, Durk?"

Durk checked a notebook."Let's see . . . Prometheus can make anything up to 40 points."

Zeus slapped the table with his huge meaty hand. "That's pretty great scorin' in my book!

"Not in mine," said Prometheus.

"Hell, you might not even *have* to shave anything. You might just have a bad day and not even get close to actually scorin' them 40 points."

"I . . . I just don't know, Mr. Zeus."

"What's to know? I don't usually offer this kind of money on a game that's not even officially college level."

Eris looked up from her book. "That's the truth."

"But I like you, kid, I like the way you play. It kind of reminds me of how *I* used to play. Besides, I hear your family needs help. I'm a family man myself. Believe me, there's nothing more important down here on this earth than the family. Don't you ever forget that, Prometheus."

"And there's the future . . . " Durk added.

"Right. You'll definitely be going to college now, and not just some shitty little community college either. I'm talkin' about a good college. The kind where I usually *do* offer some decent money, especially to those I know I can depend on . . . those with whom I've already established a workin' relationship."

Prometheus shook his head. "If I do decide to do it . . . it's got to be just a one time thing. If my mom ever found out—"

"She won't," said Durk. "She'll be too busy expanding the restaurant— the way she said your dad always wanted to do it."

"One time only."

"So be it," said Zeus.

He put out his hand to shake. Prometheus stared at it, noting both its size and the large square-cut emerald ring on the right middle finger. Then he looked around at Durk and Eris. They were both smiling and nodding their encouragement. Prometheus still hesitated another moment.

Then he shook hands with Zeus.

* * *

Hobie was watching Chang on the music camp's one real basketball court. It was strange. In the extreme. The chef was good. He moved with the same relaxed grace and power as he did when performing T'ai Chi. His whole body tone was so smooth and natural, so flexible and well coordinated with his intention of dribbling the ball down the court towards the basket. When he released the ball it was timed just perfectly and aimed dead center on target. The only trouble was that the ball never went through the net. Every single one of his shots missed the basket. Often by wide margins.

"How long you been playin' basketball?" asked Hobie.

"This first time."

"Well, you seem to be doin' everything about right."

"Except ball not go in."

"I noticed that."

"Why not go in?"

Hobie shook his head. "I don't know, but tell me . . . why are you even bothering to take up basketball so late in life when you're already so good at T'ai Chi?"

"My daughter."

"But I thought you told me you haven't even seen Chai Li for well over a decade now."

"True," said Chang, "but soon I will see her again."

* * *

Chang was counting the weeks now to the day he was going back to China. It appeared to be safe once again. He had finally gotten American citizenship and would be flying over with an American passport. In addition, his name had been on the latest list of those granted an official amnesty for involvement with Tiananmen Square. But it wasn't his safety he was worried about.

It had slowly become clear over the years that his wife's cousin's family had no intention of ever sending Chai Li to him. At first they had just stalled the issue, claiming that it was still too dangerous to move the child. Then his daughter was supposedly too sick to travel. Then one of their connections had been arrested and there was simply no physical way for them to arrange her safe passage.

As time went on, however, the stalling began to change into something else. They had managed to get Chai Li enrolled into an elite party school where she was quickly recognized as an exceptional student who soon rose to the head of the class. He was also told that she had made many new friends there and was finally adjusting to her mother's death.

Change didn't know whether to believe them or not. His daughter's letters seemed to confirm everything they told him, but that was the problem. He often suspected that they had been dictated by the relatives themselves. Her letters had also become ever fewer as time went on, while his had steadily increased in frequency. He sometimes wondered if she had even gotten them all.

Then there was the way they subtly, yet constantly, kept reminding him of his own lack of success in America. He had to agree that they were right about that. His former reputation in China had strangely availed him nothing. He'd spent years as little more than a glorified bus-boy in San Francisco's Chinatown. Moving to Philadelphia had improved his lot somewhat, but though he was cooking again even now he was still far from regaining anything like the professional status he'd enjoyed in Beijing a dozen years before. He just didn't seem to have any luck anymore. It was as if the gods themselves, or some kind of evil forces, were plotting against him. He knew it also didn't help that he'd never been able to rebound from the death of his wife and separation from their only child.

Jobs still were so few and far between and never lasted very long. That's why he was at the camp. Fortunately it looked like things would soon change. He had been promised a job in the late Fall as Chief Chef at a large new gourmet restaurant scheduled to open on the Parkway not far from the Philadelphia Art Museum. The salary there would be far greater than anything he'd ever made in either China or America. Plus there would be a full benefits package to go with it. For him and for any dependents he might have.

He told the relatives that he would be coming to see his daughter for Family Festival in September. At first they didn't even reply to this announcement, but when he wrote again giving them his flight number and time of arrival, they actually called him with gracious assurances of just how very welcome he would be. Although Chai Li wasn't available to speak with him herself, as she frequently wasn't during the rare phone calls between the two countries, they also emphasized how glad she would be to have her father come over for a visit.

Visit? They didn't seem to realize, or perhaps want to admit even to themselves, that Chang wasn't intending to go there for any mere visit. He was going to bring his daughter home with him.

*   *   *

"But what's that got to do with basketball?" asked Hobie.

"Everything," Chang replied, taking a recent photograph of Chai Li out of his wallet.

Hobie had to admit that the slim girl in the picture was really cute with her large bright eyes and long pigtails. In fact she would have probably been considered quite beautiful if there had been even a trace of a smile on her face. But there wasn't.

"Looks tall, Chang."

"Almost six feet."

"No stuff . . . really?"

"Oh yes, very tall and she lives for the basketball. That is still other reason they tell me she can't come here. She on some important regional team over there."

"So you want to learn the game so the two of you will have something in common?"

"Yes, in common. She is 21 now. Can decide to do whatever she like. I must make her want to come here. No can force."

"How do you plan to do that?"

"Simple," said Chang. "I tell her how America is best land for basketball. Only land if you really want top playing. Then I tell her all about American colleges and basketball scholarships even for women. Then I show her how in America even an old man cook like me can play game she love. I make her proud to have me for father. I show her how good I am."

Hobie put a hand on Chang's shoulder. "I just might be able to help you with that last part."

*   *   *

The basketball camp's most isolated outdoor court seemed strangely different in the faint light before dawn. It was completely silent for one thing. Even the wind hadn't yet risen to rustle the leaves in the nearby trees. Durk and Prometheus were the only people in sight as they stood directly beneath one of the baskets.

"You made the right choice, Prometheus."

"I hope so."

"The only problem now is that we've only got two weeks left to get you in shape."

Prometheus laughed. "I'm in the best shape of my life!"

"Not for that final game."

"What do you mean?"

"I mean that you've got to learn how to make it look good."

"Hey, whenever I score I always make it look good."

Durk shook his head. "Now you have to make it look good even when you *don't* score."

"Yeah . . . right," said Prometheus smirking.

"It's got to look real and natural."

"I don't know, Durk, I've never—

"Well, my boy, fortunately for you I have. So you've got a real master to teach you the finer points."

Durk tapped himself on the chest, then threw the ball to Prometheus. They played a rather relaxed game at first just to warm up, then they speeded up the action to play for real. Prometheus tried a quick lay-up and scored. Durk shook his head.

"What's wrong?" Prometheus asked.

"Everything."

"But the shot went in."

"*That's* what's wrong," said Durk.

"Damn! I forgot."

"Then watch me now and cover me real close."

He took the ball back a few yards and then went in for a fast lay-up of his own. As Prometheus moved to cover him, Durk used the opportunity to stumble over Prometheus' foot just as he took his shot. The ball still flew fairly straight at the basket, but it bounced off the rim.

"I see," said Prometheus.

"Did you?"

"Sure. That's easy,"

"Is it?"

"Sure. All you did was miss."

Durk shook his head. "Then you *didn't* see . . . at least not as much as you thought."

"You missed, Durk."

"But missing wasn't all I did."

"What else?"

In answer Durk threw the ball to him. "You try it."

They moved apart and repeated the previous action, but this time with Prometheus making the lay-up. He tried imitating Durk in tripping over his foot, but it looked crude and obvious. The ball missed the backboard entirely.

"Nobody's going to believe *that*," said Durk.

"I can smooth it out."

"Let's hope so. We've got two weeks."

When they tried it again Durk broke down the action and showed Prometheus just how to make it look like he was being tripped by his opponent. As the hours went on Prometheus slowly started to perfect the technique. Neither he nor Durk ever spotted Hobie watching them from the hill overlooking the camp.

* * *

Later that night Prometheus enjoyed himself with Eris at a party Jimmy threw for them at the motel bar. Still later he enjoyed himself with Eris alone in the cabin. She laughed when he told her how he had used Durk's tricks that afternoon in full team practice. He'd managed to fool all his team-mates who consoled him on his streak of "bad luck."

* * *

Hobie found Chang crying. The chef was sitting alone in his cabin, the picture of his daughter on the bed beside him. Her latest letter was in his hands. Mail call had come late that day and Hobie had seen Chang rush off to read the letter.

"What's wrong?" Hobie asked.

"Letter . . . from Chai Li," mumbled Chang, looking embarrassed at having been caught weeping, and quickly trying to dry his eyes.

Hobie picked up the single sheet of paper and looked over its delicately drawn characters. "I see . . ."

"Oh, sorry," said Chang, snatching back the letter, "I forget you not know our language. It is very sad message my daughter sends me."

It seemed Chai Li was now having second thoughts about her father's upcoming 'visit.' She explained to him how her new family over there might be hurt by his stay. They didn't want to tell him, but she thought it was her duty to do so. For despite his amnesty and new citizenship, it just wouldn't be appropriate to have someone like him, with his past, staying with people of position like them.

The years had been good for Jen-i's cousin and his wife. Since moving up to Shanghai he had become one of the leading businessmen in that bustling city—a real 'people's capitalist' as some put it. His economic success was bolstered by his wife's rise to the upper-middle level in the local party bureaucracy there, as well as their oldest son's recent promotion to the rank of Colonel in the People's Liberation Army.

As for Chai Li herself, the regional level basketball at which she was now excelling might well be only a first step. With the right connections there was a real chance that she could move up to China's national team in a year or two.

A lowly cook with a dissident background was hardly something that would be looked on favorably in the circles in which they all now traveled.

Chai Li didn't specifically state that she was totally against his 'visit' as such, although Chang sensed that could have well been her intention. Instead she just recommended that rather than coming to stay with them at their estate it might be better for him to check in at a hotel. There were many excellent ones in Shanghai now, and of course they would pay for it. She sounded like a travel agent as she praised both the 50-floor

Portman Ritz-Carlton at the Shanghai Centre with its elegant furnishings and outstanding health club, and the Shanghai Hilton which supposedly had the best dining in town. They could pick him up at his hotel and show him all the sights of the city. It sure sounded like she expected his stay to be no longer than a weekend.

*   *   *

"She always such good girl," Chang cried out, almost on the verge of tears again. "What happen to her?"

"Folks change," said Hobie.

"*They* change her! Make her not good."

"Maybe so. There are those who do seem to have a special knack for just that sort of thing."

"What can I do, Hobie?"

"Well . . . right now you can do this," Hobie answered, tossing Chang the basketball he'd brought with him.

The Chef just stared at the ball in his hands. "No. Not now. Not feel good."

"Let's go outside and play. That will help you feel good."

It took a little coaxing but Hobie soon had Chang out of the cabin and down onto the court. They warmed up with a bit of foul shooting, then started playing half court one-on-one. Chang had improved tremendously in such a short span of time. From that first session when he could never get a ball through the net till now when he rarely failed to do so had only been a matter of days. He was the quickest learner that Hobie had ever had. Quicker even than Prometheus had been, or any of those before him.

"You're really gettin' good," Hobie commented.

"Yeah, getting good . . . at basketball game. Just not getting any good at bringing daughter back. Too bad you can't help me with that too."

Hobie stared at Chang who was just completing a great hook shot. "You never know, son."

*   *   *

The next night saw a toughly fought game between two camp teams. The gym was packed with crowds of noisy enthusiastic fans for both sides. Prometheus played harder than ever to stack up as many personal points as he could. The idea was to establish such a scoring record that bettors would naturally assume he could easily make over 40 in the final game of the summer.

From time to time Prometheus looked up at Eris in the stands. She was always either reading or talking with someone. She never seemed to actually be watching the game, and she was long gone before it ended.

Durk ran up to him right after the final buzzer.

"Great game, Prometheus!"

"Yeah, yeah . . . where the hell did Eris go?"

Durk looked all around the gym. "Is she gone?"

"She's *always* gone. I've never seen her sit through a full game yet."

"Don't worry about it," said Durk, lowering his voice. "Hey, that was really some fantastic scoring . . . fifty-nine points tonight, fifty-six in your last game. People will really be expecting something terrific next Saturday. You really make the game look easy."

They headed for the locker room. "It's not easy," said Prometheus. "It's hard and getting harder all the time."

"What do you mean?"

"It's all that 'special' training you've putting me through. It makes it hard to play a straight game like tonight."

"Don't worry about it," said Durk. "There aren't going to be any more straight games after tonight, so you can just—"

Another player had ducked out of the gym office and was motioning to Prometheus. "Call for you."

"Who is it?" asked Prometheus, suspecting Jimmy.

"I don't know. It sounded like a little girl."

"Athena . . . ?"

"What did she want?" Durk asked.

"She said it's about his mother."

Prometheus bolted away from Durk and ran over to the office. Inside he frantically looked around for the phone, found it, then shouted into the mouthpiece. "Hello? Athena? Yeah . . . what's happening? Okay, okay. Just calm down and—"

CHAPTER THIRTEEN

DURK EXPERTLY WEAVED HIS MERCEDES THROUGH THE LATE NIGHT Chinatown traffic and pulled up to double-park beside the restaurant. Prometheus jumped out and rushed to the apartment door. Inside he found the living room crowded with mostly middle-aged and elderly Greeks and Japanese. They all nodded to him. Athena leaped into his arms and he hugged her as Emiko came up and gently put a hand on his shoulder.

"Your mother's going to be okay, Prometheus."

"Where is she?"

"In her bedroom. The doctor's still with her."

"When did it happen?"

"Right in the middle of the dinner rush. We were kind of crowded for a change so she was trying to help out with just about everything."

"I was working the cash register," said Athena.

Emiko patted her head. "Your mom seemed okay, except for looking pretty tired, but she's been like that a lot lately. Then suddenly she just fell over."

"Heart attack?"

"The doctor said no. It wasn't a heart attack or stroke."

"What then?"

"He's not sure yet."

"Why didn't you call an ambulance?" Prometheus asked.

"She wouldn't let us," said Athena.

"You mean she wasn't unconscious?"

Emiko nodded. "She was, but only for a few seconds or so, then she came to and —"

"Wanted to go back to work," Athena put in.

"Yeah," said Emiko smiling. "Can you believe that lady?"

"Yes," Prometheus answered softly.

"Well, Athena and I wouldn't let her do that, but she was firm about not having an ambulance. It was tough enough even getting her to call Doctor Okazaki, but she finally did."

"Didn't *he* recommend an ambulance?"

"Sure, but she wouldn't hear of it from him either, so he came over here."

"He still makes house calls?"

"To *this* house he does," Emiko said proudly. "You know how he was one of your dad's best friends when they were kids together in New York."

Athena made Prometheus put her down. "How'd you get here so fast, brother?"

"Durk drove me."

"Where is he?"

"Looking for a place to park."

"He's not going to find one," said Emiko, "not around here on a Saturday night."

The door to Gaia's bedroom opened and Doctor Hirokazu Okazaki came out. He looked somewhat more elderly now than he did when Prometheus last saw him over a year before, but still in great shape and very alert all the same. Prometheus remembered how the physician had a black belt in Judo. Eighth degree. He went straight to Prometheus and shook his hand firmly.

"Prometheus, my boy, how are you?"

"Fine. How's mom?"

"Well, she's resting now and she's going to be okay. It's a combination of exhaustion, stress, and anxiety, complicated by the fact that she hasn't been eating or sleeping well lately."

"Shouldn't she be in the hospital?"

"No, I don't think it's necessary just now."

"What can we do?"

"Keep her happy. Help her to relax. A couple days in bed won't hurt. You hear that, Emiko? I don't want her working."

"I hear you, doc," Emiko replied with a nod.

"Can anyone here take her place in the restaurant for the next few days?"

Everyone in the room put up their hand. Doctor Okazaki laughed and they all joined him. "I've given her all the medication she'll need tonight," he said, handing a prescription to Prometheus, "but get this filled tomorrow. I'm upping the dosage on her blood pressure medication, at least temporarily. By the way, why don't you come back to the Aikido Dojo when you get a chance? It might help your basketball playing."

When Prometheus and Athena entered their mother's bedroom they found her flat on her back with both arms laid out along the sides of her body. She looked more tired than they had ever seen her before, but she smiled when she saw them.

"Hi, mom," said Prometheus, practically whispering.

"You came? What about your game tonight?"

"We won it."

She looked confused. "Already?"

"It's after midnight, mom."

"I guess I kind of lost track of time," she said, her voice weak and fading. "The restaurant?

Athena laughed. "Is just fine. Emiko and me took care of everything . . . especially after Uncle Jason and Aunt Yoko came over to help us close up."

"How did we do tonight?"

Now Athena flashed a worried look at her brother. "Uh . . . not bad, mom, not bad at all. We actually made a profit for once."

"Thank god. How much profit?"

"I'm not sure. I didn't have time to tabulate it all yet."

"Maybe a hundred?"

Again Athena glanced at Prometheus. "Oh sure, at least that much . . . at least a hundred."

"Good."

Gaia settled back with a weary look of satisfaction on her face. Athena motioned her brother that they should leave. "Well, I hope you're feeling better," he said.

"At least a hundred," his mother murmured, closing her eyes, " . . . good."

The living room was less crowded when they came out. Those that remained were either gathered around Doctor Okazaki or talking with each other in Greek, Japanese, and English. Athena leaned close to her brother and spoke softly.

"I lied to Mom about the profit."

"It wasn't a hundred dollars?"

"It wasn't a profit," she replied.

Prometheus reached into his back pocket and removed his wallet. From it he took a single crisp bill and handed it to Athena.

"That's . . . a hundred," she said with surprise.

"Yeah, was there a loss?"

She nodded. "About eighty bucks."

"Not any more," said Prometheus as he handed her another hundred dollar bill.

"Where'd you get all this, brother?"

"I'm going to stay around for at least a few days," he said, ignoring her question, "to make sure Mom's okay, but after that I have to get back to camp for the final game of the season. It's a really important one. In the meantime, use this for whatever you guys might need around the house."

With that he counted out another three hundred dollars which he handed over to his sister. She stared at it even more wide-eyed than before, then she shook her head angrily and waved all five bills in his face. "Where the heck . . . no, excuse me . . . where the *hell* did you ever get five hundred dollars?"

"I've been working," he said, "up at camp."

"Doing what?" she demanded.

"Well, I've been helping out . . . with some of . . . uh—"

He was interrupted by his uncle Jason, a tall, bearded, bear of a man in late middle age who still spoke with a fairly heavy

Greek accent despite his forty years in America. He placed one of his thickly muscled arms around Prometheus. "My boy, I am sorry to interrupt you, but—"

"It's okay!" Prometheus said with great relief.

"There's some guy at door who says he friend of yours. Tall guy he is, with very short hair. Almost bald. Strange for such young man."

"Durk?"

Jason nodded. "That's what he call himself, but when I ask him in he say rather he would see you outside."

It was all the excuse Prometheus needed. He quickly crossed the living room to the front door and left. Athena followed him, but as she neared the door one of the relatives picked her up and started tickling her. The others all laughed in an attempt to cheer her up.

Prometheus came out of the apartment and met Durk in the dimly lit hallway. "How's your mom?"

"Resting," said Prometheus.

"She going to be all right?"

"That's what the doctor says."

"Good. I know just how worried you were driving all the way back down here."

"Yeah, I guess I was," Prometheus admitted. "Hey man, thanks for everything . . . as usual."

"What are friends for?"

Prometheus chuckled. "I'm sorry you had such a hard time finding a parking space."

"But I didn't."

"That's strange. Where did you get a space?"

"Right around the corner."

"What took you so long then?"

"I had to make a phone call."

"To who?"

"Mr. Zeus."

"Why?"

"I thought he might be able to help. I mean with your mom being sick and all."

Prometheus shook his head. "I'm sure he feels that he's 'helped out' plenty already."

"Oh no," insisted Durk, "not at all. He was very concerned when I told him what had happened."

"Concerned that it might affect his *investment?*"

"No. You got Mr. Zeus all wrong, Prometheus. He really is a family man, just like he told you. He's a nut about it, believe me. So he wants to help."

"How?"

"I'm not sure, but he said he'd meet us at the restaurant. You got a key?"

Prometheus didn't answer right away. He just stared at Durk for a time, then he looked up at the paint peeling off the hall ceiling as he considered. Finally he nodded. "Wait here."

When he re-entered the apartment he went straight over to the desk in the corner of the living room where he started searching through the drawers. Athena came up behind him. "What are you doing, Prometheus?"

"Looking for the keys to the restaurant."

"Why?"

"I've got to go down there for something."

"What?"

"Nothing for you to worry about."

"Hey, I *never* worry about things," she said, "I just take care of them."

"Good for you," Prometheus said, finding the set of keys and heading back towards the door. She followed right behind him.

"It's got something to do with the money, doesn't it?

"No, of course not."

"Then I think I'll just tag along to—"

"Stay here," he told her firmly.

"Then it *is* about the money!"

Prometheus beckoned Emiko to come over from the group that was still talking with Doctor Okazaki. Then he picked up his sister. She struggled but couldn't break free. "Emiko, can you help a certain very young lady get to bed?"

Emiko took Athena from him, her hold nearly as strong as his.

"My pleasure."

"Oh no it won't be," Athen a insisted, struggling fiercely to free herself from her aunt's grip.

*   *   *

Prometheus and Durk entered the restaurant and turned on the lights. As Durk looked around the place, Prometheus busied himself making coffee and heating up some baklava. He thought how good it was to see Doctor Okazaki again and how lucky he still made house calls. He always liked the older man who was both taller and stockier than his father had been, but who otherwise seemed so much like him. It was nice of him to extend the invitation he had made. Prometheus knew it wasn't just a matter of courtesy. He had obviously meant it. That was touching after the years that had passed.

The Aikido Dojo. Prometheus remembered how the word Dojo meant the Place to Practice the Way—or the Tao, as it was called in the original Chinese. He also remembered quite well just what the particular "Way' of Aikido was like. It was far from a happy memory.

*   *   *

For months Prometheus had been begging Doctor Okazaki to teach him Judo. He had seen the physician throwing around much younger and bigger and stronger looking men with apparent ease at a Junior High family night exhibition. Okazaki had finally relented, but Prometheus had only lasted a single night in the beginner's Judo class at the Chinatown YMCA. He never understood why.

Prometheus thought that he had followed all the instructions quite well— tripping his opponents with real speed and power, slamming them down hard on the mat with all the strength he could muster, locking their arms and legs with such force that they all almost immediately tapped out in submission. There was even that older and more muscular guy who nearly passed out from the ferocity of Prometheus' choke hold. So what was wrong?

Doctor Okazaki never told him. He just suggested that there might be a better martial art for Prometheus. Something better suited individually for him. It turned out to be Aikido. The only problem was that Prometheus didn't find it better or more suited for him at all. Just the opposite.

The fact that his own father turned out to be his instructor certainly didn't help. Not anymore than when he had tried teaching Prometheus to swim or play music. But it wasn't just that. Aikido itself wasn't what he was looking for. Sure, it had a kind of superficial resemblance to Judo with its throws and locks and holds, but that resemblance was deceptive.

To Prometheus Aikido just wasn't a real martial art at all. There was far too much emphasis on evading an opponent's strikes and on blending in with attacks in order to negate their force. Too little use of strength and power and aggression. It seemed like all the players were working together instead of competing with each other like in any other decent sport, let alone in a supposedly fighting one.

Besides, instead of just wearing straight *gis* as in Judo, there were those damn *hakamas* again just like in *Kyudo* archery. Prometheus just never felt like wearing a skirt, for any reason. To cap it all off, his father had insisted that if he wanted to learn he had to bring Athena along with him. That was just too much. Going to what was supposed to be a martial arts class with your baby sister where you got to wear a skirt and practice stepping out of the way of opponents instead of smashing them down.

Prometheus lasted longer with Aikido than he had with Judo, but not much longer. A few weeks as he remembered. It was a Friday night when he quit. His father seemed especially disappointed that they wouldn't be going to the Dojo together that night. It was as if for some strange reason he expected something out of the ordinary to happen then.

*　　*　　*

At almost the very moment that the coffee and pastry were ready Prometheus saw Zeus' black stretch-limo pulled up in front of the restaurant. Jimmy got out as his driver double-parked beside an old van. Zeus quickly walked inside and was greeted by the two younger men who were sitting at a table by the bar. "Kid, I'm real sorry to hear about your mother."

"Thanks. Have some coffee and baklava."

"So here," said Zeus, ignoring Prometheus' offering. He reached into his inside coat pocket and took out a stack of bills which he threw down on the table. "Take the rest of your money now. That five hundred advance I gave you ain't gonna last long with your mom sick. I know I can trust you to honor our deal and come through for me at next Saturday's game."

Durk laughed. "Hey Jimmy, no problem. Prometheus could score a *hundred* points if he really wanted to! Keeping it down to forty will be easy. You can count on him."

"I wasn't talkin' to you, Durk," said Zeus cooly.

Prometheus was busy counting the stack of hundred dollar bills. Durk poured Jimmy a drink at the bar. None of them were in a position to spot Athena and Emiko listening from behind the ornately carved partition in front of the door to the darkened kitchen. They had sneaked in silently from the back alley just a few minutes before.

Prometheus finished with the money. "You can count on me, Mr. Zeus."

Athena looked so shocked and angry that it seemed like she was ready to go out and start arguing. Fortunately Emiko held her back and covered her mouth.

"Just don't forget the numbers," said Zeus.

"What's to forget, sir? I'm allowed to score anything up to forty points, right?"

Zeus grinned. "Yeah. Try to make all forty of those points if you possibly can."

"No sweat, sir."

"We want to make things look good, don't we?"

"Yes," Prometheus agreed, " . . . real good."

*   *   *

It was raining lightly outside when the men left the restaurant. Zeus' driver opened the door for him. He got in and waved goodbye. Durk and Prometheus walked back towards the apartment entrance. As the limo pulled away, Athena stepped out of the shadows and memorized its license number.

CHAPTER FOURTEEN

Athena sat with Emiko by the telephone in the living room. When it rang her aunt scooped it up at once. She spoke into the phone with her voice barely above a whisper.

"Hello . . . yes . . . great."

"Apollo?" asked Athena.

Emiko nodded, then proceeded to quickly write something down on the yellow legal pad in front of her. "Okay, got it. Thanks a lot, sweetheart. See you tonight."

She hung up the phone and finished writing in the pad.

"Could he trace the license?"

"Sure," Emiko said smiling. "The limo's owned by a corporation called Olympus Enterprises. This is their address. It's uptown . . . far far uptown."

She tapped the pad and handed it to Athena.

"And that guy last night?"

Emiko nodded. "The Chairman of the Board."

"Wonderful!"

Emiko smiled smugly and then laughed. "I think so. Apollo is so smart and so good. He's going to make *Captain* of Detectives even before we get married."

Athena read from the pad. "Jimmy . . . Zeus."

"What's that?" Prometheus asked as he entered the room.

"I said Jimmy Zeus!" Athena snapped at him. "You know . . . your boss!"

"What are you talking about?

"Gambling . . . cheating by shaving points so the big shot gambler Jimmy Zeus doesn't really have to do any real gambling at all."

Emiko bowed her head. "I wasn't actually able to put her to bed like you asked."

"We heard you in the restaurant last night," said Athena, "you and your boss."

"He's not my boss!" Prometheus shouted.

"Oh no? He's the one calling the tune, isn't he? Or I should say calling the game."

Prometheus sat down on the sofa. "We need the money, sis."

"Not that badly."

"What do you know about it? You're just a kid."

"I've been doing the books, brother."

"Then you should know that it's precisely *that* 'badly'."

"Mom says we'll get by."

"How?"

"I don't know . . . but she'll think of something. She always does."

Prometheus pointed towards their mother's bedroom. "While she's like that?"

"Then *I'll* think of something," Athena insisted.

He got up and went to his sister. When he tried to hold her she resisted at first, but then she hugged him back. He patted her hair. "Maybe you will, but in the meantime we need the money just to survive."

"But Prometheus, you still shouldn't—"

There was a tear in her eye. He wiped it away. "I'm not proud of what I'm doing, believe me, Athena. I'm ashamed of it . . . more ashamed than I've ever been of anything in my whole life, but I have no choice. There's no other way."

*   *   *

Prometheus spent a long time feeding his mother as she sat up in bed smiling at him. Later he went over the books with Athena and shook his head with disappointment at nearly every entry. When he looked in on Gaia again she was sleeping so he quietly closed the curtains over the window in her room. He went down to the restaurant and worked with Emiko, Jason, Yoko, and Athena during the evening rush. After that he met Durk at the playground to practice "mistakes" like dropping the ball, 'accidentally' kicking it away when dribbling, and missing passes.

He was packing his bag the next night when Athena burst in breathlessly. She grabbed both his hands and pulled him away from the bag."I don't want you to go."

"I've got to. The game's the day after tomorrow."

"Don't play in it."

Prometheus moved away from her. "We've been through this already."

"It's wrong, Prometheus!"

"I know."

"Then don't do it."

"I have to."

"But I've been working on a plan," she said, "to make money . . . lots of money."

Prometheus smiled as he shook his head. "It's not just a matter of money. I'm committed. Zeus has got his bets down already."

"Bets against you scoring more than forty points, right?"

"Yeah."

"How many could you score if you really tried?"

"If I *really* tried? Well, Hobie once had me convinced that I could score a hundred points. Playing his way, of course."

Athena smiled. "Then just tell Mr. Zeus to bet that you *will* score more than forty."

"But don't you see, sis, the odds are better if he bets against me. Most people are expecting me to do really well, to play just the way I've been playing all summer."

"I know," she mumbled, looking down at the floor.

He finished his packing and headed for the door. "See you, kid."

It was only then that she finally looked up again. "*I* would never bet against you, Prometheus. No matter what."

"I know," he said as he exited.

*　　*　　*

Durk's car was waiting at the curb when Prometheus came out of the apartment building. Durk opened the door for him from the inside and then started the engine. Just then Gaia came out with Athena and Emiko. Prometheus looked shocked as they approached the car. "Mom! Where are you going?"

"To work," she answered.

"But you're not ready. You're—"

"Nonsense! The doctor said it's perfectly okay."

"As long as you take it easy," Emiko added.

"I will."

His mother bent down as Prometheus leaned out of the car window to kiss her. As he touched her face he looked nearly ready to cry. "See you, mom."

"Of course you will," she said, stroking his cheek, "on Saturday night. I wouldn't miss *that* game for the world!"

"But you can't!" he shouted with sheer panic in his voice. "You just can't."

"Why not? I just told you the doctor okayed me going back to work. Certainly I can sit down and relax as I watch my only son make me proud."

"Make us *all* proud," said Athena.

In desperation Prometheus turned to Durk who shut off the engine. For once Durk seemed unsure of just what to say.

"Uh . . . I'm awfully sorry, folks, but uh . . . I don't think I'll be able to drive anyone up because I'll be—"

"You've done too much for us already," said Gaia. "Besides, we have a ride."

"You do?" Prometheus asked.

"Sure. We're all going up with Apollo. You know, Emiko's new boyfriend." Athena grinned wickedly. "Yeah, you know . . . Apollo . . . the *cop*."

Jason and Yoko had just arrived after coming up the street from the restaurant. Jason nodded. "Or they could come with us in our station wagon."

"You're coming too?" asked Prometheus.

"Sure," Yoko answered enthusiastically, "and we'll have lots of room. Our kids will all be going up in their own cars or with cousin Rhea."

"The whole family?"

Athena grinned again. "Both sides."

"Of course," Jason said. "You are first athlete star we ever have in family. Everybody hearing about you for months now. You think we missing chance to see you in the action?"

Yoko walked very slowly and deliberately over to the car where she gently touched Prometheus' arm as she looked deeply into his eyes. "Your father would be so very pleased with you."

* * *

Durk expertly maneuvered his car along the night highway through light traffic and heavy fog. Neither he nor Prometheus had spoken to one another since leaving the city. Finally Prometheus shook his head and whispered. "I don't think I can go through with it."

"You damn well better!" Durk insisted.

"But you heard them. They're all counting on me."

"So is Zeus."

"But they're family."

"And Zeus is your employer who's paid you in full, in advance."

Prometheus took out the money and stared at it. "I'll give it back."

"Too late," said Durk.

"Maybe he could change his bet?"

Durk just laughed.

CHAPTER FIFTEEN

EMIKO AND ATHENA WAITED IMPATIENTLY FOR THE ANCIENT ELEVATOR TO SLOWLY make its way to the top floor of the tall old uptown office building. As soon as the doors opened and the rusty gate slid aside they dashed out and immediately started checking the names on each office door.

"Not a very classy place," commented Emiko.

"What did you expect?"

"I don't know. Apollo said this guy Zeus is a real big shot who's been around forever, so I guess I just figured—"

"There it is," Athena said pointing.

They had reached the very end of the long dimly lit hallway. The door there at which Athena was pointing was marked in fading Gothic script "OLYMPUS ENTERPRISES, INC."

Athena entered first, but found her way blocked by Nick Ares who was on his way out. For a split second the giant bald thug glanced appreciatively at Emiko coming through the door in her short tight dress, but then he focused his attention on Athena and frowned.

"What'd you want, kid?"

"Uh . . . to place a bet."

Ares snickered. "So go to a bookie."

"I thought that's just what we'd done."

"Well, you thought wrong," said Nick, shaking his head. "This here establishment's a promotional enterprises corporation, not no bookie joint."

"Sorry," Emiko said nervously, "our mistake. We'll just be going now."

She tried to pull Athena back after her, but Athena stayed frozen where she stood, looking all around the office with great interest. Her glance quickly passed over the cluttered desks, the bulging filing cabinets and the water cooler, before coming to rest on the elaborate computer system in the far corner of the room.

Nick turned away for a moment and spoke sharply to the elderly Filipino cleaning lady who was sweeping the floor behind him. "Hey, Gabriella . . . I'll be leavin' just as soon as I get these two out of here. Try to do a decent job for once, will you? Oh, and make sure you lock up and turn on the alarm system when you leave."

Gabriella nodded but said nothing as she continued her work.

Nick tried hustling Emiko and Athena out of the office, but Athena stood in place still scanning everything around her. Emiko tried pulling her again.

"C'mon. Let's go."

Finally Athena looked up at her aunt and smiled. "Okay."

As soon as they were out of the office Athena raced to the Ladies Room half way down the hall. Emiko ran after her. The rest room was dark, but when Emiko reached for the light switch Athena stopped her. When Emiko started to speak Athena put her finger up to her lips.

"What are we doing here?" Emiko whispered.

"Waiting."

"For what?"

A man's shadow passed by the translucent window in the door frame. Athena pointed at it. "That," she whispered, waiting a moment and then slowly inching the door open. She saw Nick Ares rounding the corner at the far end of the hallway. A moment later she opened the door fully and headed back towards his office. Emiko followed reluctantly.

"What's the point of all this?"

Athena ignored her aunt as they reached the office door where she knocked and called inside with the very sweetest voice Emiko had ever heard her use.

"Oh, Gabriella . . . "

*   *   *

The fog was rolling across the narrowed highway thicker than ever as Durk's car slowed down at the outskirts of the mountain town. A dark figure was walking along the side of the road just ahead. The car screeched to a halt and Prometheus jumped out.

"See you in the morning."

"Are you crazy?" Durk shouted from inside.

"Probably."

"Eris is waiting for you."

"I know."

"And do you know how far it is from here to her motel?"

"Yes," answered Prometheus.

"Then you better just—"

"See you in the morning, Durk."

Prometheus swung his bag over his shoulder and ran towards the dark figure up ahead on the road. Durk waited for a moment, then gunned his engine and roared off into the night.

Prometheus really had to sprint because the man he was after suddenly started moving away from him at much greater speed. It was Hobie. Only when Prometheus finally caught up with him did he slow his pace once again.

"How have you been?" Prometheus asked, smiling, but slightly out of breath.

"Angry."

"Why?"

"Cause I want my damn ball back!"

"I'm sorry, Hobie, but I don't know where it is."

"Look for it."

"I don't know where to look."

"I do."

"Where?"

The old man stopped and stared at him. "In the forest . . . behind the female's cabin."

"Why do you think it's there?"

"Because that's where she put it."

"If that's true," said Prometheus, "then why don't you just go and look for it there yourself?"

Hobie shook his head. "It's not my place to do that."

"But it's mine?" Prometheus asked.

"Absolutely."

Prometheus couldn't think of anything else to say after that, so they just walked the final mile into the town proper in total silence. It was finally broken by Hobie who pointed across the street at an unusually tall and muscular teenager who was staggering along the curb with a bottle in his hand.

"Do you know him?

"Uh, yeah," said Prometheus. "I think his name's Roger. He's from the camp and plays Center mostly, but sometimes Power Forward. They call him "The Enforcer." He's really good. He's—"

"Disgusting."

"Oh, you mean because he's been drinking."

"No," Hobie snapped back sharply. "I do not mean because he's been drinking. There's nothing necessarily wrong with that. I've been drinking myself this evening. He's disgusting because he can't control his drinking . . . because he's *drunk*!"

As if to prove Hobie's point, Roger suddenly stopped lurching forward. He stood in place swaying back and forth under a street lamp for several seconds, then he doubled over and vomited violently. Most of it splattered over his shoes. Somehow throughout it all he managed to hold onto his bottle.

"I see what you mean," said Prometheus.

"I hope you do, boy. You ain't been seein' much else of any sense these days. You haven't been doin' much drinkin' yourself, have you?"

"Uh . . . no, not much."

"Good. I suppose bein' part Greek and all you've probably grown up doin' a little drinkin' at home though?"

Prometheus nodded. "A little."

"Well, that's how it should be. Just a little at most. Now and then. Just a little."

"That's exactly how it always was with mom and dad."

"I'm glad to hear that, boy, but what about up here away from home . . . you ain't been gettin' drunk like that fool across the street, have you?"

Prometheus looked away. "I've been trying not to."

"Well, I hope you succeed. I sincerely do."

There didn't seem to be anything more to say on the subject so again they walked along for quite some time without talking. It wasn't until they were nearing the center of town that Prometheus thought of something.

"Say, Hobie . . . if you feel so strongly about being drunk, I guess you feel the same way about getting stoned. You know, like on marihuana?"

"You got that right!"

"Pot's even worse than alcohol."

Hobie turned his head and looked quizzically at Prometheus.

"Worse? Out of control is out of control. What's the difference?"

"Well, one's legal and one's not."

"So?"

"So there must be reason for that."

That only made Hobie snicker. "Be sure to let me know what it is when you find out."

"Hobie, do you remember that politician that I was telling you about back in Philadelphia?"

"You mean that gun-control nut?"

"Well, yeah . . . that's what you called him."

"That's what he is."

"I heard him on the radio the other night."

"What's he up to now?"

"He was talking about the War on Drugs."

Hobie stopped short and actually slapped his sides as he laughed up roariously. "The War on . . . *what*?"

"Drugs."

"What kind of war is that?" asked Hobie, his face beaming with uncontrollable mirth. "How the bloody hell can you have a war on things? Do the drugs have guns they shoot? Bombers that they attack cities with? Do those folks who are fighting drugs throw grenades at the drugs or have tanks go after them? Do they capture the drugs and make them prisoners of war?"

Prometheus shook his head. "You know it's not really a real war."

"Are you sure?"

"I mean of course it's not really a war against drugs as things."

"Correct. Like all wars it's bound to be a war against people."

"Bad people, Hobie, real bad ones."

"Some of them, no doubt."

It was just then that Prometheus felt yet another one of those strange things coming on, so he kept silent as they kept walking through the darkened town. It was only when Hobie again commented on how disgusting the drunk teenager looked, that Prometheus dared speak up again.

"If you feel that way, Hobie, then I figure you should be in favor of the Drug War."

"Son, what I'm in favor of is folks takin' responsibility for their own actions. If they get drunk or stoned or say, so sleepy and tired that they can't see straight—well, that's their business. As long as they *keep it* their business and don't go out drivin' around in their cars or flyin' planes or operatin' trains or heavy machinery. Then it becomes not their business, but the business of other innocent folks whom they're endangering."

"That's a strange attitude," offered Prometheus.

"It's common sense, boy."

"Then you don't believe in the War on—"

"On people? People who get drunk like that so-called basketball player back down the road there, or people who get stoned and nod off in their back yard or in front of their TV? No, I truly don't believe in a war on people. I'm a peace lovin' person . . . just like everyone should be."

"But what about—"

"Those who injure others? Now, them I'm against . . . but I sure don't see any need for any kind of so-called 'war' to handle them. That's what plain old ordinary everyday laws are for . . . to protect peaceful folks from those who would do them harm, not to supposedly protect them from other peaceful folks that are minding their own business."

They reached the main street of the town and turned towards the fog-shrouded train station. Prometheus kept trying to walk alongside Hobie, but somehow the old man managed to always take a step that put him just a bit ahead. At the station the Styx Cab crossed their path and the driver Al Charon waved to them.

"Want a ride?"

"I don't know," answered Prometheus.

"Real cheap just for you, buddy . . . only two bills."

"Take your ride," Hobie muttered.

He went to the cab and opened the back door for Prometheus, but Prometheus stood in place considering. Charon was laughing as he hugged a huge black dog with a spiked collar dog in the front seat with him. " Don't worry about Old C. here. He don't bite . . . much."

"Didn't Durk say that Eris herself awaits you?" asked Hobie.

"Yeah, but how did you—"

"What are you waitin' for?" Charon demanded.

Hobie nodded. "Yes, what *are* you waiting for, Prometheus?"

"I don't know. For some strange reason I guess I just kind of thought it might be more fun to hang out in town here for a while."

"More fun than that woman you got waitin' for you at the motel?" Charon hooted. "C'mon, pal, get in. Hell, I'll carry you out there for free. Just tip me a couple coins."

"What would you do here?" asked Hobie

"I'm not sure . . . maybe just follow you."

"No," Hobie said firmly. "Following me is impossible for you right now."

*   *   *

The cab let Prometheus off right at the motel cabin. He paid the two dollars Charon had originally asked for, but just as he started up the cabin's steps he remembered the tip. However, when he turned back down the cab had disappeared. Prometheus found that kind of strange because although the fog wasn't nearly as thick there as it had been in town, he couldn't even see the taxi's lights or hear its engine.

Prometheus entered the cabin and dropped his bag on the floor. He was met by Eris. Naked except for her high heels and pearls. She threw her arms around him and pressed her voluptuous body tightly against his, but he hardly responded. She pouted.

"I'm not used to waiting around for men, you know."

"Then why did you?" he asked. "In fact, just why have you stayed up here at all?"

She broke contact with him and proceeded to strut over to the bed where she lit a cigarette in its long ivory holder. "I'm on vacation."

"Just like that?"

"Just like that! I've got money. I do what I please."

"What about Epi?"

"Who?"

"Your old boyfriend. You said he was in the hospital."

"Oh, yeah," she said, stretching out full length on the bed and puckering her lips to blow out a perfect smoke ring. "You know, it's funny. He's an awful lot like you in many ways and I don't just mean basketball. He's a lot dumber maybe, but otherwise the two of you could still practically be brothers. The trouble is . . . I got tired of him."

"Just like you're going to get tired of me?"

She nodded. "If you go on like this."

Prometheus picked up his bag, swung it back over his shoulder, and turned for the door.

"Okay."

She watched in utter disbelief as he reached for the door knob. "Where are you going?"

"Camp."

In the instant he started turning the door knob to open the door she flew off the bed and rushed to him.

"Oh, baby," she pleaded, "don't leave me now . . . please."

"Isn't that what you want?"

"No."

"You confuse me," said Prometheus.

She laughed loudly. "I know. I do that."

"What do you want?"

"You!" she shouted.

She twisted both her arms and one leg around him as she kissed him deeply and passionately. This time he responded.

* * *

Emiko was worried about Athena. It was long past midnight and everyone else was asleep, but no matter how hard she pleaded she just couldn't get Athena to lie down. The child was simply too busy working away on two computers at the same time.

* * *

It was still early morning and some of the fog still hung over the motel. Prometheus emerged from the cabin and started jogging out onto the road to camp. He thought he had left Eris asleep, but she stood watching him through the window as she dialed the phone.

"It's me," she whispered into the mouthpiece. "Yeah, he just left. You did say he'll be practicing till noon, didn't you? Well, get the hell over here before then. We have to talk. There's been a change in our plans."

As Prometheus jogged he suddenly began to hear faint wisps of music drifting through the fog from the woods off to his side. It took him several moments before he could identify the sounds as that of a guitar playing variations on "Sakura," the old Japanese folk song about cherry blossoms that his father had loved so much. Prometheus stopped, listened some more, then turned and ran into the woods towards the music.

He followed the melody for a surprisingly long distance before he reached a small pond. Helen sat on a rock beside it playing her guitar. Her eyes were closed and she was smiling. She looked so incredibly beautiful, he thought, there in the faint sunlight filtering through the fog and the trees.

Hobie was nearby making fantastic looping shots up against high pine branches. All his flowing movements were gracefully synchronized with the music. He stopped when he spotted Prometheus.

"What do *you* want here?"

"I heard the music," said Prometheus.

Helen opened her eyes and stopped playing. "Hello, Prometheus."

"Hello. Please don't stop playing. It was so beautiful."

"Course it's beautiful," muttered Hobie. "That's why she stopped it when she saw you."

She stared at Hobie and shook her head. "Hobie!"

"Well, that's the way *I* sees it."

"Where'd you learn that piece?" Prometheus asked.

"Athena taught me the melody. I kind of . . . make up the variations as I go along."

"It's called 'improvisation'," added Hobie. "You ever hear of it, boy?"

"Yes," Prometheus whispered.

"Really? You mean to say you haven't forgotten everything I ever told you?"

"Not everything."

"Just my ball? Again."

"Damn!" shouted Prometheus, slapping his forehead.

He ran back the way he came, turning only once to look at Helen as she began playing again. Her hands glided so lightly over the strings of her guitar that it seemed like they weren't even making contact. In the same way he felt the very gentlest of breezes barely touching his skin as it moved her long hair back from her face. He thought it strange how in that very moment he seemed to see a kind of golden aura surrounding her whole shining body.

*   *   *

Athena was again working on two computers at once when Emiko entered her room.

"Apollo said he'll pick me up in fifteen minutes."

"Good," said Athena. "Have him get me . . . *this*!"

She hit a key and the high-speed printer started turning out page after page of material. Emiko looked at the first few sheets and frowned.

"Athena, I don't know if he—"

"And I'll need it sometime before tonight."

*   *   *

With the sounds of Helen's guitar still somehow echoing in his ears Prometheus neared the edge of the woods right behind the motel. He spotted Durk's car parked in front. Prometheus stopped short when he heard voices arguing loudly inside the cabin. He edged forward more cautiously.

Inside the cabin Eris was dressed but still sprawled provocatively on the bed smoking another cigarette in the long holder. Durk paced angrily in front of the bed.

"We had a deal, Eris. It still stands."

"Not with all the latest changes."

"What changes?"

"Zeus."

"Hey, I didn't know for certain that he was going to get involved this time . . . at least not in the beginning."

Eris smiled. "Then why did you ever set up this whole thing on the kid in the first place?"

Prometheus was listening as he crouched in the tall grass that ran all along the side of the cabin. Durk sat down on the bed next to Eris. "I'm not really sure," he said, "but I guess it was just something I thought had to be done."

"But why?"

"Maybe because Prometheus seemed to be picking up so much so easily from Hobie . . . so much of the real *magic* of the game . . . the very kind of stuff I could never get from the old man when I was his student."

Prometheus choked. Durk and Eris heard it. They rushed to the window and looked out. Prometheus pressed himself to the earth beneath the tall grass and lingering fog.

"What was it?" asked Eris.

"I don't know . . . a bird or something."

"It didn't sound like a bird."

"Who cares?" Durk shouted at her. "I'm not going to give you anything more!"

"Yes you are. You're going to give me plenty more."

"I . . . I don't know, Eris."

"You damn well better know if you really want to become one of us like you've always said."

She smiled seductively as she carefully placed one hand on his hip and the other on his shoulder. Grinding her body against his, she opened his shirt and slowly started kissing his chest. Durk laughed.

"Do you seriously expect this to work on *me*?"

"Yes," said Eris.

Durk resisted for slightly longer than she had expected, but then he clasped her to him, tilted her head back, and kissed her fully on her open mouth. A moment later he picked her up and carried her away from the window.

* * *

Prometheus quickly crawled away through the grass making his way back into the woods. Suddenly his path was blocked between two closely spaced trees by a tangle of roots, leaves, and branches. When he looked at the obstruction more closely he saw Hobie's ball peeking through it. The blue glow was just faintly visible in the forest shadows.

He pulled the sphere free and rose to his feet holding it up to the sky and twirling it above his head. Then he raced back towards the pond, laughing and crying as he went.

* * *

Athena was busy keyboarding at lightning speed when the phone rang. "Yes?" she answered. "Great! Yeah, that's okay. Just have him fax me the first part now. I can work on that while you two are getting the rest."

* * *

Prometheus neared the pond laughing and tossing the ball all around. Helen was now playing a fast Bach prelude. Hobie was gone.

"Where's Hobie?"

"Gone," she answered.

"Look what I found."

Helen smiled. "He'll be pleased."

"I hope so. I've really been pretty stupid."

"Yes."

Prometheus laughed. "You don't have to agree so quickly."

"Why not? It's true."

"Yeah," he admitted. "I guess it is at that."

"Why is it true, Prometheus?"

"Well . . . I think I made some dumb choices, but at the time I just couldn't see just how dumb they were."

She stopped playing the guitar and stared intently at Prometheus. "But you can now?"

"I think so," he said, tossing up the ball.

"Then why don't you start making some smart choices for a change?"

"Too late."

"That sounds like another dumb one," she said.

"The truth is, Helen, I have no more choices to make. I'm really trapped."

"That's tragic . . . if true."

"Oh, it's true all right. Believe me, it's true."

"I wish I could help," she said softly.

"You can."

"How?"

Prometheus pointed at her guitar. "Play for me."

"Only if you join me."

"How?"

Helen reached into her guitar case and took out Prometheus' Pan Pipes. "With this."

"Where did you—"

"Athena lent it to me."

She turned on the boom-box beside her and stared playing along with the string orchestra in the midst of the haunting Aria from Villa-Lobos' famous "Bacianas Brasilerias," No. 5. At first Prometheus just listened to the music, but then he raised the Pan Pipes to his lips and joined in, playing very hesitantly at first, but then catching the spirit of the song and playing much more smoothly and soulfully. Helen smiled up at him.

After a time Prometheus put the Pan Pipes back in the guitar case and began moving with the blue ball in time to Helen's continuing rhythm. Then he found himself dancing all around her and shooting the ball off the trees, showing the same kind of grace and beauty he'd seen in Hobie's motions. He paused, bowed, and held his hand out to Helen. "Now I'd like you to join me."

She hardly hesitated at all before she put her guitar down and got up to dance with him. They moved as one with their arms around each other as they seemed to almost fly across the grass all around the soaring cellos that came from the boom-box. Only when the piece ended did either of them really notice how very close they were to each other. Helen suddenly seemed embarrassed by the fact. She went back to her guitar and started playing along with a new song. Prometheus just stood there amazed for a moment.

Then he started dancing again by himself. He never felt freer or happier as he circled Helen. When he finally stopped he hesitated for just a moment, then bent over and kissed the nape of her neck. She quit playing and looked up at him in total shock.

"What do you think you're doing?"

"Finally making a good choice for a change," he replied.

Then Prometheus ran away, heading off in the opposite direction from which he had come. Helen watched him go. She touched her neck where he had kissed her. "Yes . . . I think you finally are."

*   *   *

Athena sat alone at the computer in her room. One hand worked her keyboard. The other held the phone as she watched sheet after sheet coming out of her fax machine.

"Yes," she said into the mouthpiece, "these are even more helpful than the last set. Just keep them coming."

CHAPTER SIXTEEN

PROMETHEUS WAS STILL RUNNING MILES LATER AS HE NEARED THE MUSIC CAMP. Running and thinking of yet another strange thing. Perhaps one of the strangest of all. It concerned Eris. Most of the guys on his team had enviously commented on how lucky he was to have a girl friend so amazingly sensual, but he suddenly realized that that wasn't really true at all.

There was actually only one sense she exuded. She *looked* fabulous. But she had no scent, no smell at all. Apart from that strange smoky one that he had later discovered didn't actually come from her body at all, but simply seemed to be in the air whenever she was around him. And somehow she didn't feel real to the touch. It was as if she was both there and yet not there at the same time. Her kisses were certainly passionate enough, but they tasted quite bland. Her words were sexy and seductive, but they were said in a voice that sounded surprisingly flat, when it wasn't outright shrill.

Helen, by contrast, not only looked and smelled so good, but she also sounded as lovely as her music, was incredibly warm to the touch, and in the single fleeting example he had had—was wonderfully sweet to taste.

* * *

Hobie and Chang Sam Fong walked out of the music camp's kitchen and crossed the parking lot to the dumpster. They were each carrying garbage bags that they proceeded to throw into the dumpster. After that they started playing basketball on the nearby court. Hobie smiled and nodded. The Chef's technique was nearing perfection. When they finished playing Chang took the ball back to his cabin. Hobie had started following him, but then stopped and turned around. He had sensed something off to his side.

It was Prometheus emerging from the woods. Both his hands were behind his back.

"Well, well, well," said Hobie. "So here you are. People have been callin' all day tryin' to find you."

"What people?"

"Durk . . . Eris . . . somebody named Zeus."

"What did they want?"

"Oh, it would appear they're just a tad worried because their star player skipped practice the day before his most important game."

Prometheus laughed. "But I didn't skip practice."

"Oh no? Well, you sure fooled them."

"I've been practicing all day."

"Not at camp, it would seem."

"No, not there."

"Okay, I'll bite. Where then?"

"*There!*" Prometheus answered, pointing back towards the woods with his left hand.

Hobie looked all around them. "Who was you doin' all this practicing with?"

"With . . . *this*," said Prometheus as he brought his right hand out from behind his back. It held the blue ball which was glowing brightly now even in the daylight. Hobie looked delighted as Prometheus threw it to him.

"You finally found it, huh?"

"Right where you said I would."

"Thank you."

"So . . . how about a little one-on-one? I was just getting warmed up today in the woods."

"No," said Hobie shaking his head sadly.

"Why not?"

"I'm sorry, son, but it just can't be."

"You won't teach me?"

"I can't."

"Ever?"

The slightest grin touched Hobie's lips but it was gone in an instant. "Now 'ever' I don't know about, but at this here particular point in time there's simply no way."

"So you're dropping me just like you did Durk?"

"No, no . . . " Hobie said with a look of deep shock on his face, "not at all like I did Durk. In fact, for exactly the opposite reason."

Prometheus stared at him. Long. Silently. "Who are you?"

"Just an old, old man tryin' to give folks the gift of a little beauty for their lives down here."

"Eris said that you're really . . . *me*."

Hobie laughed heartily from his belly. "She would say somethin' like that now, wouldn't she?"

"What did she mean?"

"Who knows? It just sounds like that gal's usual kind of confusin' crazy talk to me. After all, how can I be you? You're *Prometheus!*"

Hobie started dribbling the ball all around Prometheus, but he wouldn't let him touch it. When Prometheus put up his hand for a pass, Hobie ignored him.

"You know," Prometheus said with frustration, "it's kind of strange, but there are times when you somehow remind me of my father."

Hobie bowed. "Thank you. Teruyuki was a good man, a very good and special man."

"You called him Teruyuki?" asked Prometheus in a shocked voice.

"That was his name, wasn't it?"

"Yeah, but how did you know that? Everybody always just called him Terry."

That brought a smirk to Hobie's face. "First of all, I sure ain't 'everybody.' The man's real name was Teruyuki so that's what I called him. Wisdom starts with calling things by their proper names. A wise man once said that."

"Who?"

"Kung Fut-ze."

"Who?"

"Kung Fut-ze . . . oh, most folks know him better as Confucius —but that wasn't his real name. Kinda ironic, ain't it?"

Prometheus turned away and was silent for a moment before he looked again at Hobie. "You knew my dad?"

"I certainly did."

"He never mentioned you."

Hobie laughed. "I imagine not. Few ever do."

"Just when did you know him?"

"Oh, it must have been something like four years ago or so. I think it was around the time you were just starting high school."

"You knew me too?"

"I knowed *of* you."

"But I don't ever remember seeing you."

"That's cause you never did."

"But you and my father were . . . friends?"

Once again Hobie bowed. "I had that honor."

"That's hard to believe."

"Why?" asked Hobie as he stopped dribbling and casually took a long shot that naturally sailed right into the basket.

"Because in most ways the two of you seem so different."

"Do we now? Well, what 'seems' ain't always what actually 'is.' You should know that by now."

"Just how did you and dad become friends?"

That made Hobie laugh so much that he almost missed his next shot. Almost, but not quite. The ball spun around the rim several times before it lazily dropped in as if from sheer exhaustion. "Now *that's* quite a story."

"Tell it to me."

Hobie did.

*   *   *

It had started one cold late Autumn day in the park shortly before dawn when there was some light in the sky, but not much.

Hobie had been shooting baskets alone on the paved half-court when he spotted the middle-aged Japanese man arrive on the similarly deserted archery field nearby. Hobie stopped shooting in order to watch. The contrasting colors of the white *gi* jacket and black *hakama* skirt had immediately caught his eye, as had the long bamboo bow the man carried with a case full of similarly long bamboo arrows.

At the time Hobie found it strange how the man had immediately noticed him watching and had nodded with a smile. Most of the time Hobie found that he could observe folks forever without them having even the slightest awareness of his presence. But not this time. Not with this particular man.

Prometheus' father was in no hurry doing a long series of stretching and deep breathing exercises, followed by a period of silent meditation while he just stood in a relaxed posture staring at the target. His eyes were more than half closed and he seemed oblivious to the chilly breeze that swirled leaves all around his motionless body. By the time he finally strung his bow and nocked the first onto its string, Hobie sensed that this was no ordinary man. The swift and true flight of that arrow straight to the target's center ring only confirmed this impression. As did each of the other prefect shots that followed it. Not to mention the fact that this strange archer always turned his head away from the target even before he released each arrow.

When all the arrows in the case had been used, the man went to the target to retrieve them. Once there he turned towards Hobie to whom he smiled and bowed. Hobie bowed and smiled back.

That was the first time.

The second was about a week later when Hobie was practicing on the school playground. It was even earlier than before and a thick pre-dawn fog shrouded the empty Chinatown streets. After a fast series of lay-ups Hobie ran down to the basket at the opposite end of the court. There he set his blue ball to spinning up in air above his head. After watching it for a few seconds, he pulled it back down and spun around himself as he tossed it over his shoulder back towards the other basket. It was only when he glanced over his shoulder to watch the ball complete its long arc into the distant hoop that he noticed the man. That same small Japanese man, dressed in jogging clothes this time and standing by the fence.

Hobie felt a rare surge of surprise shoot through him. Not that he hadn't sensed *something* just before he had spun the ball up in the air, but he'd thought it was probably just a bird or a squirrel. The two were often hard to distinguish without using one's sight or hearing. He never thought it could be a man. They were never so soft and quiet. Never so smooth and harmonious and light in their movements. But this man was. Hobie smiled and bowed. The man returned both.

The third time was when they finally spoke to each other. It was early one Friday at the Chinatown Aikido Dojo. Prometheus' father was alone out on the mats practicing the unique Aikido style of rolling falls. He was having trouble centering his mind and spirit, having trouble even reaching that state of relaxation necessary to perform the art properly. It hadn't been a good day. When he and Gaia had gone over the books they realized that they were barely breaking even again. And this was the year they had really thought they'd start making a decent profit on the restaurant. To make matters worse, Prometheus had announced at dinner that he was giving up on Aikido. When asked to explain why, he would only say that he didn't like it. His father just couldn't understand that.

Just then Teruyuki's attention suddenly centered on the doorway. He sensed something there even before that strange tiny old black man appeared there. When he saw just who it was, he and Hobie both smiled and bowed to each other as they had the previous two times. Then Prometheus' father gestured to a row of metal folding chairs behind the low wooden railing that separated the entrance area from the matted practice floor.

"Have you come to watch?"

"Yes," answered Hobie, "and to learn."

Teruyuki chuckled. "I doubt that you can learn much here. I've seen you with your basketball."

"One can always learn."

"Yes, that's true. What is your name?"

With that they introduced themselves. Hobie stayed and watched the Aikido practice for the next two hours, completely fascinated by the utterly relaxed and natural way the other man moved so easily through the rushing chaos of speeding bodies all around him. When the Dojo closed the two men went to a nearby teahouse and sat talking for hours more.

Little of what they discussed that night had much to do directly with Aikido or basketball or archery. Yet, strangely all of it could apply to each of those practices as readily as it did to the actual subjects of art and philosophy of which they did speak.

Only on subsequent occasions did they each talk about their own specialty. When they did, Teruyuki somehow wasn't all that surprised to learn that Dr. Naismith's modern game of basketball was only the latest manifestation of something far more ancient. Hobie, in turn, had his initial suspicions confirmed that although Aikido in its present form hadn't been developed until the 20th Century by Morihei Ueshiba, it was actually based on timeless universal principles best expressed in Ueshiba's own formulation that the essence of his art was the loving protection of all beings.

As their friendship grew over the years that followed, Teruyuki learned little of Hobie's mysterious background apart from the names of players he had taught. On the other hand, he strangely found himself opening up as he had seldom done before with others, telling Hobie a great deal about his own life. About his joy in his wife and children and especially about his worries concerning his son.

It was shortly after that last revelation that he asked Hobie to teach basketball to Prometheus. Hobie refused. He said he never taught anyone under eighteen. When Teruyuki insisted, Hobie said he had a better idea. He would teach Teruyuki who could then teach his son himself.

The plan seemed to work well at first. Hobie had never had a student like Teruyuki. Although he had never played basketball before in his life, no one before had ever picked up the game's deepest essence and meaning so quickly or thoroughly. No one else had ever been such a joy with whom to play. Hobie taught him most of what he knew in a matter of weeks. Then it time for father to teach son.

*   *   *

Prometheus well remembered those times, starting with that vacation in the mountains when his father first introduced him to basketball—a game in which he had never had the slightest interest up until then. Looking back now, he could see Hobie in both his father's playing and in the way he taught the sport.

There was such a difference from how he had tried to teach Prometheus swimming or music or anything else.

There was such love in the way he taught basketball, such understanding of what his son wanted and needed from the game . . . and from his father. There was such respect that Prometheus actually started daring to suspect that somehow in pleasing himself he might also for once be doing something right and pleasing his father as well.

Prometheus remembered just how his father had gotten him to love basketball, and more importantly how the two of them had finally begun to grow closer to each other.

Then his father died.

*   *   *

"Tell me something," Prometheus asked Hobie several silent moments after the story ended, "why did you finally decide to teach me this year?

"That's simple. This is the year you became a man. Or least it should be."

"But why couldn't you do it right after Dad died?"

Hobie shook his head. "Cause you weren't no man then. Besides, I was far away from here on another assignment."

"What do you mean?"

"That's none of your business."

"Okay," said Prometheus, suspecting that this was one of those areas where he could never get anything out of the old man, "but I still don't understand the timing. You never teach anyone under 18, right?"

"Correct."

"But you didn't start teaching me as soon as I turned 18. You waited till months later."

"So?"

"So there had to be something else."

"There was."

"What?"

Hobie frowned. "Watching how you reacted to Durk."

Prometheus watched silently as Hobie tossed his strange blue ball into the basket once more "The game's tomorrow, Hobie."

"I know."

"I need your help."

"There's none I can offer you now," said Hobie, "except maybe . . . *this*."

The old man smiled warmly as he threw the ball back to Prometheus.

*　　*　　*

Emiko followed Athena down the darkened hallway to the offices of Olympus Enterprises. In Athena's left hand was a small box of computer disks. With her right she knocked on the office door once, then twice, then once again. Gabriella opened the door and quickly hustled Athena and Emiko inside.

*　　*　　*

Durk and Eris arrived at the motel in his car. They had been arguing heatedly there and they continued as they entered the cabin.

"And I think it's more your fault!" he shouted.

"Mine?"

"Of course. If you had only kept his interest just a little while longer, then—"

"Listen, Durk, I *did* my part."

"She really did, you know . . . " It was only when Prometheus spoke those words to them that they finally noticed him standing over among the late afternoon shadows in the far corner of the room. He kept packing all his things as he repeated himself.

"She really did, you know, Durk . . . above and beyond the call of duty."

"Prometheus!" gasped Eris. "I don't have the slightest idea what you—"

"Where the hell have you been?" Durk demanded.

"In the woods."

"What the hell's that supposed to—"

"With Helen."

Eris sneered. "You mean that mousy little—"

"And Hobie."

"Is that old fart still around?" asked Durk.

Prometheus slung his bag over his shoulder and headed for the door. Durk and Eris both stood in his path to block his exit.

Prometheus then hit the play-button on the boom-box under his arm and beautiful music filled the room. "A Love Supreme" by John Coltrane. Its effect was immediate. Durk winced, but Eris actually held her ears in pain. Prometheus laughed as he easily pushed his way past them.

"Yeah, Durk . . . he's around."

"Uh, I hope," Durk began rather tentatively, "that you haven't started listening again to any of his—"

"Where are you going?" asked Eris, still looking in pain.

"To camp."

"But darling, I thought we'd—"

"Where I belong."

Prometheus opened the door to leave, but then he turned back and walked over to the bed where he retrieved the blue ball which was glowing there. For the first time Durk and Eris became aware of it. Now they didn't even try to stop Prometheus as he crossed the room a final time and left. In fact, they backed away from him as he passed by them with the ball in his hands. They followed him, but at a respectful distance, seeming to recognize a dangerous difference in the ball now that it was with Prometheus once again. Or was the difference more in Prometheus himself now that he had reclaimed it?

Outside Prometheus walked over to Durk's car and threw something onto the driver's seat.

"What was that?" asked Durk.

"Zeus' money. Give it back to him. I'm out of the whole business as of right now."

Eris watched Prometheus stroll down the road towards the basketball camp. Her eyes narrowed. "That's what he thinks."

*　　*　　*

In the otherwise darkened offices of Olympus Enterprises Athena was working intently in the faint blue glow of the main computer's screen. Emiko stood directly behind her looking worried. The cleaning lady Gabriella sat at one of the nearby desks smiling and counting the rest of the money Athena had given her.

"We've got a problem," said Athena.

"I knew it!" Emiko exclaimed. "I just knew it wouldn't work.

Didn't I tell you it wouldn't—"

"Oh, it'll work. The trick is to get it to work at precisely the right time."

"And if it doesn't?"

"Then the whole thing is worthless."

"I knew it!" repeated Emiko. I just knew it."

Athena continued keyboarding even more furiously than ever. "For some reason the program I encoded on my virus keeps kicking in too early."

"Ladies," Gabriella said, pointing at her watch, "we must be going very soon."

"Just give me another minute," pleaded Athena.

"Okay, but no more."

CHAPTER SEVENTEEN

THE SUN ROSE BRIGHTLY IN AN ABSOLUTELY CLEAR SKY AS PROMETHEUS EMERGED from the camp dormitory and started running around the track, dribbling the blue ball as he went.

*　　*　　*

Emiko entered Athena's room to find her moving back and forth between her two computers and her printer, dashing off quick flurries of strokes on both keyboards and checking page after page of figures coming out of the laser-jet.

"When did you get up?"

"I never went down," Athena answered without turning to look at her aunt.

"You better hurry. Your mom wants to leave for camp right after lunch."

"I'm not going."

"You're not going to see your brother play?"

Athena tapped the top of the larger and newer of her monitors. "Not till I can beat this."

"But you said it was impossible."

"That was last night. I was tired, plus their equipment wasn't nearly as good as mine. *Nothing's* impossible!."

Gaia knocked on the door and called in from the hall. "Are the two of you ready for lunch?"

"Uh . . . yeah, coming," answered Emiko.

"Call Apollo," Athena whispered.

"Why? Hasn't he done enough?"

"Not yet."

*   *   *

Prometheus was working out hard with his team on one of the outdoor basketball courts. Durk sat on the sidelines mostly just watching. Twice so far he had gotten up to offer coaching suggestions. Both times Prometheus had so completely ignored him that Durk almost felt like he wasn't really there at all.

*   *   *

Gaia looked well as she stood in the center of her living room laughing with Jason, Yoko, Doctor Okazaki and many others who were all just getting ready to depart for their big trip up to the camp. "Where's Athena?" she asked Emiko who was just entering from the hallway.

"Uh . . . she's feeling kind of bloated from lunch."

"We should wait then."

"I can take a look at her," offered Doctor Okazaki.

Emiko waved her hands at both of them. "Oh no . . . no, I'll just take her for a little walk to help her digest all that sushi, then I can drive her up later with Apollo."

"That sounds good to us," Yoko said, helping Jason herd an impatient brood of kids towards the door.

Jason nodded his ready agreement as he checked his watch. "Yes, let's get show on road."

They all left. At the sound of the door closing after them, Athena came into the living room carrying her box of variously colored computer disks. "Is Apollo on his way?"

"Yeah," answered Emiko.

"Good. I'll call Gabriella."

"She's not going to like this."

"I know," said Athena. "How much money do you have?"

*   *   *

Prometheus was exercising alone on one of the Nautilus bench-press machines in the weight room. Durk burst in, looking very ill at ease. He was followed by Jimmy Zeus and Nick Ares. Zeus threw his money down on the chest of Prometheus.

"What the hell is this supposed to be?"

"Your money," said Prometheus.

"No, kid . . . that's *your* money! Don't forget it."

"I'm giving it back."

"No deal. I don't *want* it back. You know what I do want, and I damn well better get it. Just what is it you're plannin' to do tonight?"

"Play basketball," said Prometheus.

"And how many points are you plannin' to make?"

"As many as I can."

Zeus grinned evilly. " As long as there's no more than forty of them."

"Who knows?"

"*You*, punk! You're the one that damn well better know," Zeus shouted, pressing down on the bar and adding his own considerable weight to the 180 pounds of iron Prometheus was already resisting. "My bets are in, so get it straight . . . if you shoot more than forty points . . . we shoot you!"

Durk tried pulling Zeus away from the weight bar, but Ares held him back. The bar was nearly pressing into Prometheus' chest now. "Hey, Jimmy," pleaded Durk, "there's no need to talk like that. Maybe we could just—"

Suddenly a whole team of players entered the weight room and started exercising at most of the available stations. Jimmy and

Nick moved away from Prometheus. Zeus laughed long and loud as he led Ares and Durk out of the room. As a parting shot he pointed his index finger like a gun at Prometheus. "Have a good game tonight, kid . . . up to a point."

* * *

By late afternoon the camp parking lot was quickly filling up. Prometheus was crossing the lot when he spotted Jason's car pulling into one spot while carloads of other relatives were circling behind him. Gaia got out of the car and approached her son. "I want to talk to you, Prometheus."

"We got lots of time for that," he said, kissing her cheek. "You're early."

"But you're glad I'm here?"

"Of course, Mom."

"Good. That's one of the things I want to talk to you about."

"How are you feeling?" he asked.

"That's another," answered Gaia.

Prometheus started walking everyone across the parking lot towards the cafeteria where he had been heading. "Do you suppose we could do all this talking while we eat? I don't want to have anything too close to game time."

"I suppose we could," his mother answered.

"Say, where's Athena?"

"She was feeling a little sick after lunch. Emiko will be driving her up later."

"I hope so! She's really going to like what she sees me do tonight."

Before they were able to leave the parking lot they were greeted by still more carloads of other relatives driving in.

* * *

Like the night before Emiko stood directly behind Athena as she worked away at the Olympus Enterprises computer. This time, however, Gabriella was pacing nervously by the door. She knew Zeus and Ares were gone, but she didn't know just when they might be back. She wondered if she could have gotten even more money from the child.

Suddenly Athena banged both her hands down on the computer table, just missing the keyboard in front of her. "Damn!"

"Athena?" asked Emiko.

"I've run into another safeguard . . . a really good one this time too."

"Do you think you—"

When the door slowly started to open Gabriella was nearly startled to death, but then she relaxed a bit when she saw Emiko smile and go running to the man who was entering the office. It was Apollo; tall, handsome, and with the very same kind of dark Latin charm that Gabriella herself had always found so greatly attractive in a man. He looked all around the place and then slowly shook his head.

"I don't know exactly what's going on here, Emiko . . . and like I told you before, from what I *do* know . . . I know enough to know I don't want to know any more."

"Huh?" said Gabriella.

"What's your point?" Athena asked without turning her attention away from the monitor.

"My point is that it's time to get out of here."

"Si, I agree," urged Gabriella.

Athena resumed working.

"We'll miss the game," Emiko told her.

The keyboarding proceeded at a furious pace. "Let me just try one more thing . . ."

* * *

Prometheus and his mother were sitting together at a small circular table in the camp cafeteria. Jason and Yoko and lots of kids sat nearby at a larger table. The rest of the clan were in booths along the closest wall.

"Yes," said Gaia, nodding her head, "you're absolutely right."

"You mean about being wrong?"

"Right."

"Then all along," asked Prometheus, "I've been wrong?"

"Right!"

"Dad never thought I was stupid . . . that I just couldn't do anything right?"

"Never."

"But I always thought—"

"You were wrong, son."

"And what I'm thinking about now?

His mother touched his cheek. "It's right."

Prometheus held her hand to his face. "I miss him so much I could cry."

"So cry."

"Why . . ." Prometheus began, afraid that that's exactly what he was going to do right there in front of everyone, " . . . why did he have to die . . . so young, so strong and healthy?"

"Who can explain the fates, Prometheus? He had been out jogging that morning just like he did every morning. He was proud of that. Doctor Okazaki said your father was in better condition than most men twenty years younger than he was. He had covered several miles along Kelley Drive like always, then had circled back to Chinatown. It was still so early. Why would . . ."

Prometheus held his mother as her shoulders began to shake and tears formed in her eyes as they just had in his own. "Why would," she went on, "there be a long black limousine at that time of day in our neighborhood? What business could it possibly have had turning the corner of our street . . . striking your father down right in front of our restaurant, then speeding off without ever even slowing down to see if he could be helped?"

Gaia's whole body was shaking now as her son held her even tighter. He shook his head, knowing there were answers to such questions. It was simply the fates as she had said.

"I'm sorry," she said, wiping her eyes. "I try so hard to not let it get to me . . . especially for your sister's sake, but sometimes the memories just come back too strongly for me. That damn limousine! I can still see it driving away. If only I could have gotten its license number. Maybe then the police could have found it. There are even times when I think I see it again. Times like tonight when I thought I saw it parked outside the gym here, but I know that's crazy. Those things all look alike."

Prometheus looked deeply into his mother's dark eyes and knew he had to change the subject. "Tell me about Eris."

Gaia laughed. "What's to tell you? You're obviously a lot closer to her than I am."

"No," said Prometheus. "I mean the original Eris . . . the one from the Greek myth. Hobie said you would know."

"You should know too, son. I remember telling you and Athena all the old myths years ago."

He frowned. "Somehow I've forgotten. Please tell me again."

"Well . . . okay, let's see . . . Eris. You know it's strange how that girl is named after her. I've never known another child to be given that name before."

"Why?"

"Because the first Eris was the goddess of confusion and strife. The Romans called her Discordia, the goddess of discord.

She wasn't good in any way. What modern parent would want to burden their daughter with the same name as such a creature?"

"Where did she come from?"

"Some say her mother was Hera, who as Zeus' wife was the Queen of the Gods, but most think Eris was the daughter of Nyx or Night, who in turn was the daughter of Chaos.

"The most famous story about Eris, and the one most characteristic of her, took place at the wedding of the lovely sea goddess Thetis and a mortal named Peleus. Eris disrupted things with a golden apple inscribed with the words "for the most beautiful." She rolled it across the floor and watched as other goddesses all fought to claim it as their own.

"They then asked the most handsome man in the world to judge among them. His name was Paris. Each of the goddesses tried to bribe him to choose them. They offered him wealth and power and wisdom, but in the end he picked Aphrodite."

"What was her bribe?" asked Prometheus.

His mother smiled. "The love of the most beautiful of all mortal women on earth."

"Hey, that doesn't sound so bad."

"Oh, but it was! The woman was already married to a man named Menelaus. When she left him for Paris he went after them with his brother Agamemnon. The result was the Trojan War."

"Who was the woman who fell in love with Paris?"

"Her name," said Gaia, a worried look crossing her face, "was . . . Helen."

*　　*　　*

By early evening the music camp was nearly deserted. Most of its inhabitants had already left for the game across the lake.

Helen sat alone on her cot in the empty cabin waiting for Hobie to pick her up. Chang Sam Fong offered them a ride over in his car and Hobie had agreed to help the cook finish cleaning up the dining room. They said they'd be at her cabin in half an hour, so

Helen decided to use the time to practice.

She was playing Francisco Tarrega's classic tremolo study "Recuerdos de Alahambra" when she caught a glimpse of a shadow passing by outside the window. The scent of strong musky perfume drifted in on a strangely cold breeze for such a hot night. A moment later Eris entered the cabin.

"What do *you* want here?" demanded Helen.

"To help you, my dear."

"With what?"

"*That,*" Eris replied, pointing at the guitar.

"What do you mean?"

Eris smiled. "You're good . . . really quite good, but you've got a long way to go to be really great."

"I know."

The older woman smoothed out the thin silk of the short black cocktail dress that clung so tightly to her voluptuous body, glancing with just a bit of disdain at Helen in her simple white camp shorts and t-shirt. "It could take you years, Helen . . . many many years."

"I know that too. What of it?"

"It could . . . but it doesn't have to."

"What are you talking about?"

"Just that you can have it all right now . . . tonight!"

"How?"

"I can give it to you."

Helen shook her head and laughed, then she shivered just a bit as Eris reached down and touched her guitar. "I'm quite serious."

"Do you play?" Helen asked nervously.

"Just watch . . . and listen."

Eris snatched up the guitar and sat down on the cot across from Helen. She strummed the strings a few times, then frowned and proceeded to re-tune them.

"What are you doing?"

"Tuning up," sneered Eris. "You're almost a quarter-tone off. How can that be?

"Well, the piano room is closed and I seem to have lost my tuning fork."

Eris laughed mockingly. "Piano? Tuning fork? Don't you have perfect pitch?"

"No," Helen replied softly. "My teachers say I have excellent relative pitch, but it's not quite—"

"Poor baby! Well, that's something else I can give you."

Eris then began playing scales. Slowly at first, but then rapidly increasing in speed until her long slender fingers were flying up and down the finger-board barely touching the frets as each digit sailed across the strings. She sat absolutely still and unmoving, a look of utter calm on her face in the midst of the sonic storm she was generating. Then she grinned wickedly as the velocity reached a point where the scales sounded more like lightning-fast arpeggios, and then went beyond even that till they blended together into what sounded like solid 8-note chords strummed with a single stroke.

Helen was amazed. And a bit horrified. She had never experienced any-thing like it before. She was certain that not even her current teacher, a re-nowned master guitarist from Spain, could begin to match what she was now hearing. It was unearthly. It was unreal.

"That's im . . . impossible," Helen stammered. "No one can play like that."

Eris chuckled. "Wrong. Anyone can . . . if I teach them."

Helen turned away to look out the window, hoping to see Hobie coming. He wasn't. "They were just scales."

"Right," Eris readily agreed. "How about some real music then . . . say that Tarrega piece you were struggling with."

Helen was forced to turn back and stare at her guitar as Eris made its sounds shimmer with the sureness of her touch. The difficulty of the piece lay in the constant tremolo effect that required one's fingers to ripple over the strings as the thumb played the melody and embellishments.

Any good guitarist could do it, but only those with extraordinary technical facility could produce a tremolo with the right dynamics so evenly paced
that each fluttering finger touched its string at precisely the right moment.
All the great guitarists of the 20th Century had used the song as a showcase of
their virtuosity and Helen had enjoyed recordings by each of them. She especially liked the interpretations by Segovia, Julian Bream, John Williams, and
Christopher Parkening. She thought the best of them all, however, was Liona
Boyd whom Helen felt had mastered the technique almost to perfection.

Now she was forced to change her mind. Even the tremolo of her favorite
guitarist came in second to what Eris was now demonstrating right in front of
Her. There was no 'almost' involved with the perfection of technique Eris had
achieved.

"Can even your Liona Boyd do this?" Eris asked Helen as if reading her
mind.

"No."

"Can any of them?"

"No."

"You're goddamn right they can't. Only *I* can . . . but you can too, if you
want me to teach you."

Again Helen looked a out the window. It was really getting dark now and
Hobie was still nowhere in sight. "What would it cost me . . . my soul?"

"What?" Eris screamed, visibly shaken and nearly choking as she abruptly
stopped playing, but then she quickly composed herself and smiled again at
Helen."An interesting idea, but no . . . it will cost you very little. Hardly
anything, in fact. Just a simple little favor I'd like you to do for me."

"What kind of favor?"

"Oh, just a little something I'd like you to ask your boyfriend."

"I don't have a boyfriend," said Helen.

"Don't try to be coy with me," Eris snapped back impatiently. "I'm talking about Prometheus!"

"But he's not my—"

"He certainly is! Why else would he ever leave . . ." Eris stopped to consider for a moment, then her growing frown changed back to her more usual
smile. "Wait a minute . . . are you still a virgin?"

Helen was thoroughly embarrassed. "That's certainly none of you business."

"Oh, but it is . . . *my* business as well as—"

"No it's not."

"So the two of you really haven't slept together yet? This is even better than any of us expected."

"Get out of here!" Helen shouted.

"Without even telling you what I want you to ask Prometheus?"

"I don't care. Just get out!"

Eris showed no sign of getting up as she continued to caress the guitar with both her bejewelled and manicured hands. "I only want you to ask him to honor his agreement with Zeus."

"What agreement?"

"To not score more than 40 points in the game tonight."

Helen's whole body began to shake and then stiffen as tears came to her eyes. "I would never even think of asking him any such thing."

"Why not?"

"Because it's wrong!" replied Helen, completely flabbergasted.

"So?"

"So it's wrong and he would never do such a thing anyway."

"Oh, I think now that he just might . . . if you were to, so to speak . . . 'sweeten the pot'."

"What do you mean?"

"I mean if you were to offer him your virginity if he did what you ask."

"You're crazy!" cried Helen, her head swimming so badly that she had to lay back on the cot and close her eyes. "This whole thing is crazy. After all, it's only a basketball game,"

"Oh no," Eris countered. "It's so much more than that."

"Go away!"

"Without giving you the gifts of perfect pitch and perfect velocity and perfect tremolo?"

"I don't care," shouted Helen. "I don't want them. I don't want anything from you."

Another strangely cool breeze stirred the trees outside the cabin window, then blew across Helen as she lay on her cot. She opened her eyes. Eris was gone. The guitar lay on the other cot. A moment later Hobie appeared in the doorway.

"Ready to go?"

Helen got up and went to her guitar. Hobie noticed the tears on her face and he gently touched her shoulder. "Are you okay?"

"I . . . I guess so."

"Were you asleep?"

"I don't know."

"Well, you kind of look like you had a bad dream or something."

She placed the guitar back in its case and then slid the case under the cot. Hobie went out first. She followed him, locking the cabin door after them. The car was parked at the bottom of the path to the cabin. Chang had the engine running and the headlights on even before they reached it. A few minutes later they were pulling out of the music camp grounds on their way to see Prometheus play. The two men sat up front talking basketball while stared out the back window at the reflection of the full moon on the lake.

She was thinking of Eris' strange offer and wondered why that woman felt she'd even consider such a deal. Why would she ever be willing to give up something of value to do something wrong? Something of negative value. Eris must have thought her terms would be tempting, but why? Helen smiled to herself. She knew she would always choose to earn her accomplishments rather than be handed them as a gift.

Besides, the gift was far from being what Eris obviously thought it was. Sure, the sheer flawlessness of her technique was quite astounding—but astounding in the way things could be at a freak show. But worth anything in return? Anything of importance? Certainly not. Eris' technique was perfect, but only in the way a machine or a robot could be said to be perfect. It wasn't truly music at all. It was far too cold. Too calculated. There was no passion in it. No heart or soul. No warmth at all. That was really strange.

*　*　*

Apollo's customized van had little trouble cutting through the traffic on the way up to the camp. His attention was focused on the road as Emiko and Athena turned to face each other in the swivel chairs behind him.

"But you're still not sure?" asked Emiko.

"No, not really. I did my best. It's a good virus . . . the best I could create, but who knows? If it works, then it works. If not, then—"

"Then Prometheus is in big trouble."

Athena nodded. "He is anyway."

CHAPTER EIGHTEEN

THE BIGGEST CROWD OF THE ENTIRE SUMMER WAS ENTERING THE CAMP GYM AS a storm slowly gathered in the night sky above them. Inside Gaia sat with all the members of her extended family who could possibly attend. Eris was sitting with Zeus, Nick Ares, and other assorted hoodlums. Durk led his players out onto the court and the crowd erupted with deafening cheers. However, just a moment later even this noise was drowned out as the storm outside intensified with truly frightening cracks of long rolling thunder.

Helen sat between Hobie and Chang. She waved to Prometheus. Hobie flashed him a quick 'thumbs-up' sign. The buzzer sounded and the game began. Prometheus received the ball from his team's center and he was on his way towards the basket, moving with all the grace and beauty of his best times with Hobie, gliding in and out between opposing players almost as if they weren't really there.

He scored.

The board read: HOME 2 VISITORS 0

The other team came back strong. Their players were all acting in the same way Prometheus had when he'd previously played them . . . sneaking in every kind of foul whenever they thought they could get away with it. Before long Prometheus was bruised and bloodied.

Despite this, however, and despite the fact that he kept passing the ball off to his team-mates much more than he ever had before, he still managed to make the majority of his team's baskets. Some of those scoring shots were magically long three-pointers that somehow seemed to actually float out of space and time on their long flight to the basket. Others were equally magical rebounds where Prometheus also appeared to be playing in an entirely different space/time continuum altogether than everyone else on the court.

The crowd loved it. They thought it was rapidly turning into one of the finest nights of basketball they'd ever witnessed, despite the fact that increasingly numbers of the spectators were starting to worry about the storm outside which raged as they could never remember a storm doing before.

Durk looked increasingly concerned as Prometheus continually got hurt, yet refused to fight back. Zeus hardly watched the actual play of the game on the court, but he constantly checked the score-board to follow the course of the action that mattered most to him:

HOME 9   VISITORS 4
HOME 16 VISITORS 12
HOME 28 VISITORS 25
HOME 39 VISITORS 37
HOME 51 VISITORS 49

Prometheus was suddenly struck hard by an elbow to the nose that knocked him flat. The referee blew his whistle. The teams lined up for Prometheus to take his foul shots as Durk came running out with ice and a towel.

"Are you okay?" he asked as he tended Prometheus.

"I will be."

"You don't have to take all this crap, you know?"

Prometheus smiled at him. "I know."

"You could fight back . . . like I taught you."

"I know."

"It wouldn't be like you were . . . " Durk hesitated," . . . hitting *first* or anything."

Now Prometheus smiled even more as he patted Durk's shoulder. "Really?"

"What the hell do you think you are, Prometheus . . . some kind of god or something?"

Prometheus laughed. "Sometimes you never *do* know."

Then he laughed again as Durk left the court. Prometheus dribbled a few times before shooting. He scored both fouls with ease. Play then resumed, but the buzzer sounded soon afterwards, ending the first half.

HOME 53 VISITORS 49

In the stands Zeus turned angrily to Eris. "He scored *thirty-seven* points . . . in the first half!"

"So?" asked Eris, totally bored.

"That means he can only score three more points in the whole rest of the game!"

"So what are you going to do about it, Jimmy?"

Zeus grinned.

*   *   *

He entered the men's room right behind Durk. They stood alone together at the urinals.

"Take him out," said Zeus.

"What?"

"He's injured, ain't he?"

"Well . . . yeah," Durk conceded, " . . . a little."

"So take him out."

"But he's going to be okay."

Zeus cocked his right hand like a gun and put his index finger up to Durk's head. "Oh no he ain't. Either you take him out now or *I* will later."

"Uh, it will look bad if I do it right now," said Durk.

"I don't care."

"Let him at least start the second half."

"Why?"

"So he can score those last three points he has coming to him."

"Nah, that's too dangerous. He might go over . . . even by a single point."

"Then suppose I yank him just as soon as he scores anything . . . one, two, or three points. Just let him play some more."

Zeus looked at him funny. "Why are you talking like this? What's it matter to you?"

Durk thought hard for a moment before he answered. "I don't know."

The game resumed. Prometheus continued moving just as well as he had in the first half, but he was even more of a team player than ever; frequently passing the ball and hardly ever shooting. On the rare occasions when he did shoot, he failed to score.

Zeus smiled at Nick who smiled back at him.

The scoreboard showed the ever tighter course of the game's action:

HOME 53 VISITORS 51
HOME 53 VISITORS 53

HOME 55 VISITORS 53
HOME 55 VISITORS 56

Zeus kissed Eris. Helen looked at Hobie. The old man simply shook his head slowly.

A team-mate passed the ball to Prometheus. With absolutely no hesitation whatsoever he immediately fired off an incredibly fast shot. The ball flew right through the hoop. The crowd roared.

HOME 57 VISITORS 56

Durk immediately signaled for a substitution. He sent in another player for Prometheus, who left the court looking completely mystified. "What are you doing?" he asked Durk.

"I'm uh . . . worried about your nose."

"My nose is fine now," Prometheus insisted. "What are you *really* doing?"

"Saving your life."

Prometheus watched glumly as his team faltered badly without him. The opposing team was soon dominating most of the game's action. A player on their squad zapped in an extra long three-pointer.

HOME 57 VISITORS 59

Then just a few moments later

HOME 57 VISITORS 61

Gaia whispered something to Jason who just frowned and shook his head. The play continued unmercifully for Prometheus' team.

HOME 60 VISITORS 66
HOME 68 VISITORS 84
HOME 73 VISITORS 93
HOME 75 VISITORS 98

Just then a blinding bolt of lightning struck a tree near the gym. All the lights went out. The only illumination inside the gym now came from moonlight streaming through the windows and a few flashlights and cigarette lighters in the crowd.

An official made an announcement. "Please remain seated. We should have emergency power fairly soon."

Nick turned to his boss. "Well, it sure looks like everything's okay now."

"I'm not so sure."

"What'd you mean? Durk came through, didn't he . . . when he pulled the kid?"

"Let's not take any chances," said Zeus.

He pointed at the tallest player on the visiting team who was getting a drink at the water fountain in the beam of someone's flashlight.

*　　*　　*

Prometheus was in the locker room arguing with Durk when Nick entered waving his hand towards outside. "Yo, Durk . . . Mr. Zeus wants to see you."

Durk immediately headed in the direction Nick was motioning. Prometheus tried to follow, but Ares blocked his way.

*　　*　　*

Out on the court Eris intercepted the tall player on his way back from the water fountain. She spoke to him very briefly, then led him off to one of the darkened offices nearby.

*　　*　　*

The wind and rain finally seemed to be dying down as Durk made his way across the parking lot to where Zeus was standing beside his long black limousine.

"I'm not happy," said Zeus.

"Why? I pulled him just like you said."

"Yeah, but I was thinkin' about that funny way you were talkin' before. You wouldn't be havin' any second thoughts, would you?"

"Hey, Mr. Zeus . . . you know you've always been able to depend on me."

"Just make sure he doesn't go back in. If he does, then you share in his misery. Would you like to go back livin' in that lousy little dorm room on that lousy little scholarship?"

"No."

"On the other hand," said Zeus, "just keep him out, and I'll double this at the end of the game." He tossed a stack of bills at Durk who caught the money, but then just stared at it like something alien.

"Ain't you gonna count it, kid? There's a couple grand there."

*　　*　　*

In the darkened office off the court Eris was counting out a handful of hundred dollar bills. She folded each one of them in half. Then she pulled up her dress and tucked the money into the top of her black stocking. "This will be waiting for you," she said, stroking the inside of her thigh and flashing him a glimpse of her sheer panties above " . . . *all* of it."

*　　*　　*

Zeus had left the parking lot and gone back inside the gym. Durk stood standing beside the limo. He was staring at the money he'd been handed.

"Lot of cash there, boy," Hobie whispered, approaching from behind.

Durk spun around startled. "*You?*"

"A lot more than I ever could've got you."

"It wasn't money I wanted from you," said Durk.

Hobie nodded. "That's true. What you wanted was power . . . which is much worse."

"Power to play better."

"Better than other *players*, you mean?"

"What was wrong with that?"

"There's no beauty in it," Hobie said.

"Oh yeah? Well you never gave me a chance to find that out for myself."

Hobie considered this. "You may be right about that. Patience has never been one of my virtues."

"Except with Prometheus."

"Son, I guess you really *are* right ."

"So what do you want now?"

"To give you that chance," said Hobie, reaching out and gently touching Durk's forehead.

The last time he'd done that was at Durk's wedding. A strange wedding. A wedding without a bride.

*　　*　　*

Durk had always been taller and better looking than most other boys his age. The girls had all liked him ever since grade school. Since Junior High many of them had been absolutely crazy about him. So much so that their parents were often worried about it. They never suspected that there was actually no reason to do so. Durk never even thought of taking advantage of any of the girls. He was much too shy. Their advances only scared him away.

There had been one girl in his sophomore year of high school that he liked. A small Vietnamese girl named Lacey who was at least as shy as him. It had taken Durk a full year to get up the nerve to ask her out. Unfortunately, she didn't have the nerve to accept.

After that he concentrated all his time and energy on basketball until it became his whole life. He attended his Junior Prom with his cousin, and his Senior with the daughter of a family friend. It was only in his Freshman year of college that he ever started dating.

Her name was Margit. She was an exchange student from Poland and she was beautiful. Tall and blonde and most importantly a basketball player herself. A basketball player who moved with the very ease and grace that he was trying to bring to his own game. Durk was smitten from the first.

Though hardly shy at all like Lacey, Margit wasn't pushy or forward like so many of those other girls who had turned Durk off over the years. Soft spoken and serious with the clearest blue eyes that seemed to light up in his presence, she was refined and cultured and so much more knowledgeable about most things than anyone he had ever known.

With her sweetly clipped accent she introduced him to Bach and Beethoven and Mozart and Rachmaninov and of course Chopin. She got him drinking cappuccino and champagne, aroused his interest in ballet and foreign films. They read Shakespeare together, as well as Goethe and Schiller, Victor Hugo and Balzac, Mark Twain and Jack London, Ayn Rand and Jack Kerouac. They spent hours at the Philadelphia Art Museum which he had visited only once before on a grade school field trip. Hours more at the nearby Rodin Museum whose very existence he'd never before even suspected.

Their first date had been in early September. By Thanksgiving they were living together. He proposed to her on New Year's Eve. The wedding was set for June, right after school ended. Many of the members of her large wealthy family would be flying over for the event. They were all nominally Catholic, but had no objection to the civil ceremony that Durk and Margit preferred.

Durk's parents were absolutely astounded by the size and style of the reception that was to immediately follow in the ballroom next to the hotel chapel. They were told to invite as many from their side as they wished. A big band had been hired to play all night, and there was to be a full course sit-down dinner for everyone.

It was Margit's mother who first discovered that her daughter was missing. Both families had stayed at the hotel the night preceding the wedding. Less than a half hour before the ceremony was to begin Margit had excused herself to go back upstairs to her room. She needed to change her stockings. When she failed to return her mother had gone after her. She didn't find Margit. She only found her letter.

It was addressed to Durk. He read it first to himself, then shared the gist of it with both sets of parents. Neither he nor they could understand it. She wrote that she loved Durk and always would. She was sorry that she had to hurt him and everyone else who had come for the wedding, but she just wasn't ready for married life. She begged them all to forgive her for having waited till the very last minute to make that decision. She wished Durk a happy life.

Margit's parents were devastated. They didn't know what to say to Durk. Strangely though, he seemed to be taking it all in stride. So much so, in fact, that he actually offered to help them out. He'd heard Margit's industrialist father complaining to her uncle the politician about the huge cost of the affair. They'd have to take a loss on nearly all of it since so many things had been paid for in advance, and it was far too late to cancel most of those that hadn't.

Durk told them in that case they should go ahead with the reception and let everybody have a party since it was already paid for. He then paid them out of his own money for the cost of the honeymoon. He intended to go on it without Margit.

Some of the relatives on both sides were shocked at the idea. Other guests were worried about how Durk could ever hold up for the night. These included Hobie who paced the hotel hallways in his shiny black tuxedo that looked so similar to his usual suit. He had been teaching Durk since his senior year in high school.

Strangely the reception turned out to be better than anyone could have hoped for, given its circumstances. The band was great and the food was magnificent. As for Durk, he ate and drank more than anyone and he danced more than he ever had before in his life. When the reception was over he packed his bags, thanked Margit's parents for a wonderful time, and proceeded to take a taxi to the airport. They were all amazed at how he didn't seem to be at all sad. Thankful that he didn't appear angry.

Of course he was filled with both emotions. As his plane flew south towards the Caribbean honeymoon resort each vied for dominance within him. At first it was the sadness that seemed so overwhelming. Margit gone. Forever. He loved her so. He needed her so much. But then the anger became a greater contender as he read her letter over again . . . especially the one part he hadn't mentioned to anyone else.

It was the part where she wrote of their relationship together. She explained that while she had no real complaints about him, somehow there was something missing. He had often made her happy. To an extent. She knew how much he adored her, worshiped her, did everything he could to please her. And in most ways she had been pleased. But in some strange way it was things like his very kindness, gentleness, thoughtfulness and honesty that had finally given her doubts about wanting to spend her life with him.

The letter admitted that she really couldn't explain it any better, but it was somehow as if . . . as if . . . hell, as if he were too good for her.

Too good? Durk whispered angrily, his face filled with rage in the darkened first class section of the plane. What could that possibly mean? How could he, how could anyone, ever be too good? That didn't make any sense. It was a contradiction in terms. Wasn't it?

His anger was then quickly overtaking him when suddenly the sadness returned and he remembered all their good times together. All the love. Or at least what for him was love. The battle continued throughout the flight and on into that first night in the luxury beachfront suite where he sat alone drinking rum and alternating between fits of tears and fits of angrily punching the empty bed and its pillows.

All that changed the next day. It was then that he met someone who would change his life. Despite all the rum he simply couldn't sleep. He left the hotel before dawn and wandered aimlessly down the deserted beach. It was several miles from the resort when he finally stopped and looked out over the ocean. A woman was swimming alone far off shore. He watched as she turned and headed towards him. It was only when she eventually stepped out of the high rough surf that he realized she was naked. And stunningly, aching gorgeous. Her whole magnificent body appeared golden as it glistened with sea water.

Without saying a word she went right to him, put her arms around him and kissed him passionately. Then she took his hand and placed it on her breast. Moments later they were making love on the sand in the first faint light of the new day.

When Durk first woke up he was sure it must have been a dream. Things like that just never happened in real life. Besides, he was now lying in his bed at the hotel, not on some beach miles away. But then he turned over and there she was. Sleeping right beside him. Just as naked. Just as golden. She awoke then and they made love again. And then again and again throughout the day.

They also talked. She wasn't just as beautiful as Margit had been, She was also just as smart. Maybe even smarter. She spoke very little about herself, but got him to tell her everything. Not only did she seem to identify with all the hurt and anger and humiliation that he felt, but she also showed him ways to fight back against it. She showed him how he'd been such a sucker all his life. Not just with Margit, but with everything . . . even basketball.

She convinced him to change his whole way of life. To stop being such a chump. Such a patsy. To start thinking more about himself. A whole damn lot more. To start doing things for his own benefit for once. She convinced him, but he still couldn't exactly see how he could change so completely. She answered that she had a friend who could help. His yacht was anchored just out beyond the reef.

Durk agreed to meet her friend, hardly even noticing the strangeness of both their names. Hers was Eris. Her friend was Zeus.

*   *   *

The lights finally came back on and the game continued. Both teams were playing terribly now. There were lots of missed shots, incredibly poor team-work, and a nearly complete lack of any sportsmanship or style. Prometheus' team kept trying to out-muscle their opponents, but they simply didn't have the size or power to do so.

"We're losing!" shouted Prometheus.

"So we lose," Durk said. "So what?"

"It's not right."

"What? That we lose?"

"No, not just that. It's not right . . . any of it. It's not right . . . period!"

Durk glanced up at Prometheus who was sitting in the row just above his. Then he looked up at Hobie who sat up higher still. Durk noticed how the old man was listening intently to every word between Prometheus and him. "What do you mean?"

"*That*," said Prometheus, pointing out at the court. He was distraught and nearly in tears. " . . . the whole way the game's being played."

"I can't put you back in. Zeus would kill you."

"I'll take my chances."

"There *are* no chances with him," Durk warned. "He's a man of his word, believe me."

"I don't care!"

"You'd actually risk your life?"

"Yes."

"For a game of basketball?"

"For what it can mean," said Prometheus, "for what it can stand for . . . yes. For the deep beauty it has when it's played right . . . when it's good and truthful. Yes, for that I'd risk anything. Wouldn't anyone? Wouldn't you?"

There was a brief moment before Durk replied. When he did so, his voice was but a whisper. "If I send you back in . . . you'll only be going into hell."

"All right, then," Prometheus said with a grin, "I'll *go* to hell."

Durk again looked up at Hobie who was smiling now and nodding his head. Zeus reacted with both anger and horror when he saw Prometheus re-enter the game. He quickly whispered to Eris who then signaled the tall player she had bribed.

That player now concentrated all his efforts solely on stopping Prometheus from scoring, even to the extent of giving up his own chances of making points. Despite this, Prometheus still succeeded in changing the nature of the game. He consistently stole the ball from his opponents and passed it off to his team-mates. Unfortunately, they still couldn't seem to score. The game appeared to be going nowhere. At a lull in the crowd noise, Hobie stood up and started chanting. "Prometheus Go . . . Go! Prometheus Go . . . Go!"

At first the old man was ignored, but as he continued his chant it started to be picked up by others. First by Helen and Chang, then by Gaia and all her relatives, finally by complete strangers all throughout the gym. Soon it was thundering from everywhere.

"*PROMETHEUS GO . . . GO! PROMETHEUS GO . . . GO!*"

Athena was just entering the gym then with Emiko and Apollo. They immediately joined in the chant.

Prometheus grabbed the ball and headed down court at terrific speed. The tall player was waiting there for him. He sneak-clipped Prometheus so expertly that he wasn't even called for a foul. With his mouth now even more bloodied than his nose had been before, Prometheus looked up at Hobie who was continuing his chant as he raised the blue ball above his head. It wasn't glowing any longer. It was shining! Like a brilliant blue star. Far brighter than Prometheus had ever seen it before.

Prometheus smiled. In the space of a single moment he was remembering all he had learned from Hobie. Not just about the game of basketball, but the old man's strange views on slavery, racism, guns, the politics of left and right, and drugs as well. He realized how all of it could be summed up in those two words Hobie had given him when he touched Prometheus' temple with his hot index finger . . ."be good."

That was all Prometheus had ever really wanted from the beginning . . . to be good and to maybe someday do something right for a change, something that would count, something special. He looked down at the gold watch on his wrist. That was strange. He had hardly worn Helen's gift since she had first given it to him. He'd never worn it before when playing basketball. Yet tonight, in the most important game of all, he had slipped it on without even thinking about it. What was it Helen had said? It would help him know what time it really was. He realized now that was true. It was also reminding him of when it was either too late . . . or not too late.

Prometheus rushed the tall player as if he was going to crash through his defense, but at the last possible instant he stopped, stepped backwards to the side, and shot for the basket. The ball sailed right through the net without even touching the backboard or the hoop itself.

The crowd roared. As soon as they settled down again Hobie resumed the chant, now waving the blue ball in time with the rhythm.

"*PROMETHEUS GO . . . GO! PROMETHEUS GO . . . GO!*"

Everyone in the stands immediately joined back in again in full force. Zeus smacked Nick Ares in the head. Hard.

"Hey, boss, it ain't my fault. I'm real sorry you lost so much money."

"*Money?*" Zeus screamed at his henchman. "You damn idiot! What the hell does money have to do with it?"

"But I thought because you lost so much you'd—"

"Of course I lost so much, but it ain't the money I'm talking about."

"Uh, what then?"

Zeus smacked him again. "Nick, you been in this role just a little too long. Look around us. *That's* what I lost . . . and it's a damn lot more than any amount of money."

Nick Ares looked around them. What he saw was the crowd in the stands and the players on the court . . . just people . . . ordinary people . . . happy and joyful decent human beings sharing the incredible beauty of the game and glad to be on the earth at least in that one strangely magical moment.

Eris gestured wildly to her tall player who stood frozen in place looking confused. Durk started cheering as strongly as anyone.

The game went on. Prometheus now did most of the scoring for his team, but they all soon caught his spirit and began playing with much of the same grace he exhibited. Often he'd pass to his team-mates, but increasingly they just smiled and sent it back to him.

The scoreboard kept recording history:

HOME 86 VISITORS 104
HOME 88 VISITORS 104
HOME 91 VISITORS 104

As play continued another transformation was taking place—the opposing team also started playing in the pure style being shown by Prometheus and his team. The tall player stopped trying to cheat. He began scoring again, as did both his team-mates and those of Prometheus. Everyone was moving around the court with the most extreme grace and agility. It was as if they were all dancing to some strange unheard but deeply felt music. The sheer level of everyone's play was soon ascending to something approaching nearly supernatural heights. It was becoming the greatest basketball game ever played on earth.

While the speed, coordination, ball-handling skills, and general performance of each player neared absolute perfection, the crowd's chant now dropped Prometheus' first name in favor of a single word.

"*GO . . . GO . . . GO . . . GO . . . GO!*"

Paradoxically, as their mantra rocked the building it was Prometheus himself who was scoring basket after basket now.

HOME 111   VISITORS 114
HOME 113   VISITORS 116
HOME 115   VISITORS 118
HOME 118   VISITORS 118

There was no special reaction from anyone as Prometheus tied the score. They were all too caught up in the game itself. The officials left the court and stood on the sidelines cheering away like everyone else in the stands. Eris, Nick Ares, and even Zeus himself were standing and cheering too.

Time ran out and the buzzer sounded, but it could hardly be heard above the chanting crowd. In any case, it was completely ignored by everyone as the action continued on the court. The lights were flickering on and off now, creating a kind of strobe—effect as they alternated with renewed lightning flashes outside the gym.

In the glow of one flash Hobie's shirt rode up as he raised the blue ball above his head in cadence with the cheer. On his flesh was a ragged old scar over the area of his liver. People around him in the stands stared and pointed at it. Hobie just nodded and smiled. Prometheus looked up at that same instant and saw something just as strange as the scar. Hobie's eye-patch was now covering the other eye. The newly revealed eye looked just as big and just as good as the previously uncovered one. But there was one exception. Instead of being blue, this one was brown.

The game ball went out of bounds. Hobie instantly threw in the blue ball to replace it. No one objected. Prometheus caught the ball right under the opposing team's basket. He was quickly surrounded by that team's players. He jumped straight up high above them and seemed to stop there for an instant frozen in both space and time. He spun the ball on his finger, then moved the finger away and watched happily as the ball continued spinning on its own in mid-air just as it had done for Hobie. Prometheus then took the ball back in both his hands and fired off a full-court shot.

The blue sphere seemed to float towards the far away basket in slow motion. The crowd's chanting reached an absolute crescendo and the building shook as never before. In the instant that the ball dropped into the basket all the lights went out and the lightning ceased.

CHAPTER NINETEEN

I T WAS A CRISP BRIGHT DAY AT THE SCHOOL PLAYGROUND. A PERFECT DAY FOR shooting hoops. Not that any day wasn't perfect when it came to basketball. Hobie was teaching Prometheus and Durk out on the court. Athena sat nearby watching them.

With her was the Vietnamese girl Lacey. She had been at the game to watch her cousin play on the team opposing Prometheus. Durk had literally bumped into her in the parking lot after the game. They had a lot of catching up to do and they had done it in the town's only all-night coffee shop. Durk found that she was no longer as shy as she used to be, but she was just as lovely. She had just completed her B.S. in only three years at the University of Pennsylvania and would be starting medical school there in the Fall. And no, she had said with a far from shy smile, she wasn't currently seeing anyone. And yes, she would meet him back in Philadelphia at their old playground.

No one noticed as Zeus' limo pulled up at the curb. He got out alone. Nick Ares was nowhere to be seen. Neither was Eris Yin. Everyone kept playing basketball.

"I want to talk to you," Zeus shouted as he walked over to the court. " . . . *all* of you."

"Why?" asked Durk, dribbling the ball. "You didn't lose anything."

Hobie snickered. "Perhaps because he didn't gain anything either . . . not with the game being officially declared null and void."

"*Official* don't mean anything to the people I deal with, pops."

"You mean . . . you did lose?" asked Durk, suddenly concerned.

Zeus stared at each of them in turn. "It's strange, ain't it . . . nobody even thought about that one way or the other last night, did we? It was like we was all hypnotized or some kind of thing . . . like somehow it didn't matter."

"Yeah," Durk agreed. "I know exactly what you—"

"Well, it *matters*!" snapped Zeus.

"How much did you lose?" Athena asked, walking up to the big man.

"Nothing, kid, nothing at all."

Durk shook his head. "But if the null and void ruling doesn't mean anything to the gamblers—."

"It doesn't!"

"And you bet that Prometheus wouldn't score more than forty points—"

"That's how I placed my bet."

"Then since he certainly did score more than forty points . . . how could you not lose?"

"Simple," said Zeus. "My bet got changed."

"They let you do that?"

"I wasn't the one who changed it."

"Who did?"

"I don't know. It was all done by computer."

Athena turned away to hide her grin.

"How was your bet changed?" Durk asked.

"To favor Prometheus scoring *over* forty points."

Durk stopped dribbling and handed the ball off to Prometheus as he faced Zeus more fully. "But lots of people thought he would. You couldn't have gotten good odds on a bet like that . . . certainly not as good as you could have the other way."

"Better," said Zeus.

"How?"

"The trick was in just how many points my bet said he'd go over forty."

"And how many was that?"

"Sixty."

"You mean your bet—"

"My bet was changed to him scoring a hundred points! Just like he did."

"Yeah . . . " Durk mused, " . . . a bet like that could really get you some great odds."

"Especially since I was the only one who bet that way. Oh, there was one other, but that was some chump change bet that hardly affected the odds at all."

Athena started to laugh, but she quickly covered it. She then edged her way over to Zeus' limo. Making sure that the others weren't looking, she counted out five hundred dollars from her back pack and threw the money on the car's front seat.

Durk was laughing. "So you actually made more money than you expected?"

"Lots more," said Zeus.

"So you're not angry?"

"No, I'm plenty angry. I'm angry as all hell. I don't like people breakin' deals with me, and I don't like no computer tricks . . . but somehow money has a way of soothin' some of that."

Hobie eyed him suspiciously. "Then what do you want here right now?"

"Just a chance to show my gratitude, pops, that's all."

Zeus removed a huge wad of bills from his suit jacket and held it out in front of him. Durk and Prometheus stared at the loot. It was far more money than either of them had ever seen before in their lives, even their lives with Zeus.

"No thanks," said Prometheus. "I've already gotten offers for full scholarships at three different colleges."

Zeus only smirked. "Scholarships, huh? Durk here will tell you just what they're worth. Won't you, Durk?"

"Sure," said Durk, "they're worth . . . everything. Absolutely everything you'll need."

"Have it your way," Zeus mumbled, shaking his head,"See you boys in the Fall."

"Not if they see you first," Hobbie muttered.

"Well, I guess I'll be going now," said Zeus as he started walking back towards his limo.

Hobbie nodded. "Just make sure you *keep* going."

Zeus stopped and looked back over his shoulder. He was grinning. "I will, Hobbie, I will . . . until next time." Then he added something that Prometheus found exceeding strange."Zaijian, daihuir jian . . . because wo yiding lai."

Prometheus didn't speak all that much Chinese, but he knew enough Mandarin to know that Zeus had said 'goodbye, see you later because I'm definitely coming.' But coming where? What did he mean?

"You know," Zeus said, addressing Hobie, but answering Prometheus's own unspoken question, " see you soon on *Zhongqiu Jie*."

The traditional Chinese Moon Festival in early September?

The day of family reunions? What the devil did Zeus mean by that?

Oh well, thought Prometheus, it wouldn't matter anyway. Hobbie had said he'd be out of the country for a while just before then. So Zeus wouldn't be finding him anywhere near Philadelphia after all.

It still seemed to bother Hobie though. "Zou kai!" he shouted at Zeus, ordering him to go away . . . which he finally did.

That also seemed strange to Prometheus on two counts. He didn't know the old man knew any Chinese . . . and he didn't remember Zeus and Hobbie ever actually meeting before. So how did Zeus know his name? And what were the two of them doing conversing in such fluent and colloquial Mandarin. A Mandarin tinged with a decidedly marked Shanghai accent?"

Prometheus and Durk resumed playing. This time going two-on—one against Hobie and finding themselves unable to even get near the smiling oldster. Lacey got up to help the boys. A few moments later Helen arrived with Gaia. Athena jumped into the game. Then Gaia too joined her children in their play.

That didn't seem at all strange.

www.ingramcontent.com/pod-product-compliance
Lightning Source LLC
Chambersburg PA
CBHW020610250626
47154CB00004B/1442